KIDNAPPED IN
KEY WEST

KIDNAPPED IN KEY WEST

Norah-Jean Perkin

Susan Haskell

ABSOLUTELY AMAZING eBOOKS

ABSOLUTELY AMAZING eBOOKS

Published by Whiz Bang LLC, 926 Truman Avenue, Key West, Florida 33040, USA

For information contact:
Publisher@AbsolutelyAmazingEbooks.com
ISBN-13: 978-1501005817
ISBN-10: 1501005812

KIDNAPPED IN KEY WEST

CHAPTER ONE

Key West, Florida

Something about the flower girl's unblinking gaze unnerved Robyn Locke more than it should have.

Robyn had managed to overcome last minute jitters and nightmares of her first disastrous marriage. She'd overlooked the argument outside the church between her husband-to-be and father. She'd even kept her cool in the face of oppressive heat and humidity and her father's ill-advised joke about changing her mind. Despite it all, she had walked down the aisle at Saint Mary Star of the Sea and married Will Ryder, the man of her dreams.

So why, only hours away from the end of the day, was she letting the big-eyed stare of a six-year-old freak her out?

Robyn pushed her veil away from her face. "Uh, sweetie, is there something you want?"

The little girl's brown eyes didn't waver, but she held out a pudgy hand. In it was a paper folded into a neat two-inch square.

"For me?"

The child nodded, handed over the paper, and left without a word. A veteran of five weddings, Will's little cousin Carly had sailed through the day's events with an aplomb Robyn hadn't come close to matching. Even Carly's blonde hair and coral satin dress had come through

1

the muggy May weather in better shape than those of the other female members of the wedding party.

Beside her, Izzie Sudak, Robyn's maid of honor and best friend, shook her head. "That kid's so together it's scary. Like something out of a spooky movie."

Robyn smiled tightly, relieved she wasn't the only one unsettled by Carly.

Izzie stood up and yanked down the skirt of the coral gown that clung to her ample curves in all the wrong places. Her updo had come undone, and hung in frizzy spirals around her face and down her neck. Dark sweat marks had formed between her breasts and under her arms. Robyn suspected she was in much the same shape, though her ivory off-the-shoulder wedding dress was more forgiving, thank God.

Robyn was lucky she was able to have her reception at the beach venue she so desired. Key West being the second most popular wedding destination after Vegas means the desired dates were hard to come by.

Izzie wiped the perspiration from her neck with a coral colored linen napkin. "Mind if I desert you? It's got to be cooler standing up. And I want a word with Vince."

Robyn laughed. "Sounds like a plan. Right now I feel like I'm stuck to the chair."

Though nightfall had come early, precipitated by the heavy cloud cover, the air remained thick and oppressive. Without the aid of air-conditioning, the one hundred and twenty-five wedding guests and the wedding party – with the exception of Carly – were visibly wilting in the Key West tropic spring heat wave. A flowing canopy under the moonlight on the shore of Key West's South Beach had sounded so romantic, but in reality was turning out to be a debatable choice this time of year.

As Izzie walked away from the head table, Robyn unfolded the square of paper and flattened out the creases until she could read the hand-written note.

I'm so sorry about everything. Please meet me outside by the pool bar. I need to talk to you. Laura.

Robyn frowned. Sorry? About what? Laura Rennick was one of her employees at Island Fit, the health club she'd bought after her mother died. Laura was a personal coach and Crossfit trainer. She'd been invited to the wedding, along with her auto mechanic boyfriend Craig; in fact, she was the one who'd suggested the tent for the reception.

Robyn glanced around. Most of the tables were still full, though some guests had strolled to the lapping water's edge in hopes of a breeze. Now that she thought of it, she didn't recall seeing Laura or Craig anywhere today. Izzie might know; she managed Island Fit. But she was already at the other end of the tent.

Robyn crumpled the note in her hand, stood up, and pulled the flowing silk skirts of her dress away from her damp legs. Going to the pool to see Laura was a perfect excuse to stretch. Besides, she was worried. Why had Laura missed the wedding?

As she made her way around the head table, she scanned the tent for her husband. The moment she found him, standing by a table talking to two of his three elderly maiden aunts who had driven in from Miami, her breath caught and familiar warmth filled her chest. Will's third aunt had recently fallen in her home and broken her hip so she could not attend. They usually travelled as a pack.

At six feet, Will Ryder towered over his tiny aunts, the contrast in size making his lean, athletic build all the more evident. He had discarded his black tuxedo jacket and rolled up the sleeves of his dress shirt. The soft lighting illuminated his shock of blond hair and the bronzed planes of his strong, angular face. He looked far more relaxed and natural now than the strained, pale-faced man waiting for her to join him at the altar a few hours earlier. Her father's bad joke and disdain for Will's work as a building contractor aside, this was the man she loved and whom she knew – yes, knew! – loved her back.

Holding her skirt above her ankles, she picked her way through the tables, stopping only to lay a hand on Will's muscular arm. She rose on tiptoe and whispered in his ear. "Hey, hot stuff. We still on for tonight?"

Will pulled her close. His electric blue eyes took on a wicked gleam. "Wouldn't miss it for the world, Mrs. Ryder." Then his lips brushed hers, with the promise of more to come.

She grinned and wriggled from his grasp. "I'll be with you soon."

Spirits higher than they'd been all day, she fended off requests to stop and talk as she skirted the side of the reception tent and made her way to the pool bar and searched for Laura. The clatter of dishes and raised voices spilled out from the tent in the distance.

Then she saw Laura. She was standing by the pool gate, her silvery-white ponytail and light clothing just visible in the glow from the parking pavilion sconces and the hotel rooms above it. She gestured for Robyn to come over.

Holding her dress higher to keep it from dragging on the pavers, Robyn passed the pool bar and approached Laura. She started to smile, then stopped, shocked at the woman's drawn and anxious face.

"Thanks so much for coming over," Laura said. She looked around furtively. "I was afraid you wouldn't want to talk to me."

"Why wouldn't I talk to you?" Robyn frowned. "And why aren't you at the reception?"

"You still want me at your wedding? After what's happened?"

"Why wouldn't I? What's –"

A muffled scream, followed by shouts and a crash interrupted her. She turned back to see the reception tent wobble and then collapse.

"What –"

A black-gloved hand slapped a sweet-smelling cloth over her nose and mouth at the same moment something stabbed her arm. She struggled to escape being dragged inside the parking structure, but it was already too late.

≈≈≈

One moment Will Ryder was discussing the merits of putting a second floor on Aunt Marcy's tiny cottage, the next he was scrambling to prevent a listing tent pole from crashing into the seventy five-year old's head.

He grabbed the pole just as the overhead decorative lights went out. Screams, breaking glass, curses and laughter filled the air, along with the smell of spilled beer, wine and spirits. The heavy weight of damp canvas hit his head and shoulders, muffling the sounds and smells around him. With a shock he realized that what the rental people had insisted was impossible had happened; the tent had collapsed.

Struggling to keep the pole from hitting the ground, Will called out for his best man, who was also his older brother. "Vince?"

"I'm right here." Vince's strong voice came from only a few feet to his left.

"Help me lift this pole. If we can get at least this one up high enough, people should be able to see their way outside."

A moment later Vince stumbled into him. Working together they managed to push the pole, weighted down by heavy white canvas and billowy facade, to an almost upright position. Faint light spilled into the tent through the entranceway, illuminating the dark shadows of people, overturned tables and chairs.

Will silenced the bedlam with a piercing whistle. When the noise faded, he commanded everyone to stay calm and to leave by the exit opposite to the head table. He cautioned everyone, "Watch for any broken glass and if you've got a flashlight in your car, get it and bring it back here."

The chorus of voices rose again. Guests calling for their friends and relatives. Parents searching for their children. Will added his own voice. "Robyn?" he shouted. Then again, louder. "Robyn! Where are you?"

From just behind him, where the head table had been set up, came Izzie's voice. "She went outside just before the tent collapsed."

Then Izzie was at his elbow, along with a cloying cloud of apricot scent. "Most likely in the washroom."

Will heaved a sigh of relief.

He shifted his hands on the metal pole and Vince groaned. "What's this tent made of? Lead?"

"Feels like it, doesn't it?" Will squinted into the darkness, trying to make out individuals. "Dad? Raul?"

The familiar voices of first his father John Ryder, and then the slightly accented tones of Robyn's father, came from nearby.

"Go out and see if you can figure out what happened to the tent," Will said. "And find Robyn."

"Sure."

"Of course."

Slowly the tent emptied. Will felt around with his foot, but couldn't find a base for the pole. "D'you have any idea where the footing for this pole is?"

"No. Actually, I don't think these poles have footings. They're just stuck in the sand."

A flashlight flickered at the opening to the tent. "Anyone still in there?"

"Mark!" Leave it to his younger brother to be first back with a light. A lawyer, Mark always seemed to be prepared. "Bring it in here so we can see what we're doing."

Mark crawled through the opening, then made his way to where Will and Vince held up the pole.

"Can you see a base for this pole?"

The beam of light traversed the area just in front of the portable dance floor. Mark raised the light to Will's face. "Nope. Doesn't seem to be one."

7

Guided by the flashlight, Will and Vince wedged the end of the pole against the wooden platform dance floor. With the top of the pole still attached to the tent, it stayed upright, if not stable.

The three men made their way to the exit. As Will pushed aside the canvas, he was met by the bizarre sight of bobbing flashlights, dozens of people milling about and talking loudly, some of them still drinking, their clothes crumpled or stained. Someone had maneuvered up to the gate in the hotel parking lot so the headlights were directed at the fallen tent. John, his father stood to one side, his jacket off and shirtsleeves rolled up. A length of nylon rope dangled from one hand.

"At least half the ropes on two sides have been cut, son. And the extension cord from the power source."

"Cut?" Will's first thought was of Robyn. Fresh worry sliced through him.

"Yeah. Most of the ropes along the side of the tent facing the ocean. At the side, too." His father grimaced, then pushed his wavy graying hair out of his face.

"Where's Robyn?" demanded Will.

"Raul went looking for her." The older man stopped abruptly. Will followed the direction of his gaze.

His new father-in-law appeared around the side of the fallen tent. Raul Leopoldo looked nothing like the immaculately dressed man who had walked Robyn down the aisle only a few hours before. The wealthy Argentinean's bow tie had come undone and hung around his neck like a piece of limp spaghetti. His dress shirt was partially unbuttoned and his cummerbund had ridden up his abdomen. But what struck Will hardest was the fear that animated the man's face and his coal-black eyes.

Answering fear clamped around Will's heart. "Robyn – where is she?"

The antagonism that had marked the two men's relationship as recently as this afternoon flared in Raul's dark eyes, then went out. The older man's lips thinned, and he spoke as if each word hurt. "No one out here has seen her. But we found an unconscious woman by the stairs in the parking pavilion."

He paused. "And we found this." He held out a torn scrap of paper.

Will stared at it, his mouth suddenly dry. After a moment he reached for it.

At first, the typed words made no sense. He read them once, twice, and a third time, before they finally formed into a coherent, chilling message:

Give us $1.5 million or Robyn dies.

CHAPTER TWO

" . . . son?"

Will stared at the words in disbelief. How could . . .

He swallowed hard to dislodge the lump of fear that had settled in his throat. "Robyn's been kidnapped. They . . . they want one-and-a-half million dollars. . . or they'll kill her."

"Let me see that." His father reached for the paper.

"Don't touch it!" Vince ordered. "It's already got two too many sets of prints on it." The former police officer took the white handkerchief from the pants pocket of his tuxedo, draped it over his hand, and took the paper by a corner.

The action galvanized Will. He pulled his cell phone out of his pocket.

"What are you doing?" Raul tried to wrench the phone from his hands.

"What do you think? I'm calling the police."

"No!"

Everyone stared at Raul.

With what looked like a colossal effort, the man pulled himself together. He cleared his throat. "I've had experience with kidnappers in South America. On more than one occasion my companies have had to ransom mining executives and other personnel in Argentina, Colombia, and Brazil. It's usually best not to involve the police."

"This isn't Argentina," Will snapped.

"Please." The older man placed his hand over Will's. Will looked up. He saw his own fear mirrored in Raul's dark eyes.

"Please," he repeated. It's my daughter. After all these years without her, I don't want to lose her again. We all know this isn't about you. It's about me. I'm the only one here who could possibly come up with that kind of money."

The comment about money grated, but Will's antagonism faded. He understood exactly how the man felt. Still, he shook his head. "I'm sorry, Raul. You're not the only one who loves Robyn."

He handed his phone to Mark. "Call 911. Get them to send an ambulance for that unconscious woman, too."

He turned back to Raul. "Now show us where you found this note."

For a moment, Raul looked as if he were going to raise more objections. Then his expression flattened and his shoulders sagged. "Come with me."

He turned and grudgingly started for the parking area.

≈≈≈

Dawn had begun to chase the night from the sky by the time Will, Vince, John and Raul made their way to the parking lot a hundred yards from where the tent had been erected. In addition to a couple of police cars, only hotel guest vehicles remained in the lot. Most of the wedding guests had departed hours ago, after giving statements to the police.

At the edge of the lot, Will stopped abruptly and sucked in his breath.

The silver Cadillac Coupe de Ville he'd rented for the wedding loomed before him, a horrifying reminder of everything this day should have been. White, coral and yellow paper flowers, bedraggled now after the downpour that erupted just as the police arrived, bedecked the perimeter of the windshield and the sides and trunk of the car. Soggy streamers in matching colors hung from the back of the roof, their bright colors bleeding into a gaudy "Just Married" banner stretched across the rear window.

Without a word, Vince ripped the banner down, along with most of the sodden streamers. He turned to Will. "Give me the keys."

Will's hands closed over the keys in his pocket. He shook his head. "I can drive."

"No way, Will. You look like the walking dead."

"He's right, son. You've had a terrible shock. It's better if —"

"I'll drive," Will snarled. He popped the doors and stalked around to the driver's side. He not only could drive, he *needed* to drive. Anything to take his mind off the fears swirling around in his head. Where was Robyn? Was she okay? Who took her? Anything to provide even the semblance of control, however illusionary, in a life that had spun out of control in the last few hours.

To his relief, no one argued further. He turned on the car as his father and Vince got in the back seat. Raul took the front, beside him.

Will's stomach tightened in resentment, but he quelled it. He couldn't let the dislike he'd felt towards Robyn's father since day one color his actions now. Too much was at stake. Raul had insisted on accompanying him home, and Will knew he was right. Besides, the older man was clearly hurting every bit as much as he was. Robyn was his daughter, his only child, a child he hadn't known for most of her twenty-eight years.

And now she was missing. Kidnapped.

Will jammed his foot onto the gas pedal and sped out of the lot onto South Street through the light at Simonton in search of anyone who might have seen anything. The roads were close to deserted, and he cruised slowly up and down the Old Town streets, up to White Street and the NOAA office then down United to the Truman Naval Station then across Whitehead past the Lighthouse and Hemingway House. After so many hours of inaction, of standing around helplessly while the police did their thing, all of it frustrated by darkness and rain, fatigue and too many people, it felt good to be moving. To be doing *something*.

No one spoke during the drive. After a few minutes, soft rhythmic snores emanated from the back seat. Will glanced in the rearview mirror, not surprised to see his father had fallen asleep. The old man had been going to bed before ten for years and by rights should be getting up about now, but worry over Robyn had kept him awake and on edge. He was crazy about his new daughter-in-law, and her disappearance had hit him hard.

Will welcomed the quiet, though it did little to calm his churning thoughts, or prevent him from reviewing again and again what had happened. Even before the first uniformed officers had arrived, he and Vince had found a Silent Rider ATV abandoned at the base of Simonton its engine still warm. A chain had been run from a trailer hitch on the rear to a loop in the downed tent's roof. Someone had used the ATV to pull the tent down, after conveniently cutting the ropes on two sides.

Will had recognized the unconscious girl immediately. It was Laura Rennick, one of the fitness instructors from Robyn's club, Island Fit. Izzie pressed the skirt of her dress to the bloody gash in the back of the woman's head while they waited for the ambulance to arrive. It only occurred to Will now that Laura hadn't been attired for a wedding. Instead she wore a tan tank top and Capri pants. But wasn't she supposed to be a wedding guest? Laura and her boyfriend?

Mark's flashlight ranging over the parking pavilion had turned up one more clue before the police arrived – one more clue that Robyn had been taken by someone against her will. Caught on the stairway railing was a scrap of ivory lace – the same lace that edged the short veil framing Robyn's face. Then the uniforms arrived, followed shortly by a detective from the Monroe County Sheriff's Office and a short but punishing downpour. One look at the note and the unconscious woman, and they were on the phone to the FBI. The guests not already driven into their cars by the rain were herded away from the tent and of course hung out at the pool bar until they were questioned. After what seemed hours, the Criminal Investigation Division had blocked off the area, set up spotlights, and began combing the beach, pool area and parking areas for anything connected to Robyn's disappearance.

All for nothing, as far as Will could see. The rain had lasted no more than twenty minutes, but it had come down hard, likely washing away any potential evidence. The K-9 unit was coming in at first light to see if they could pick up the trail, but would it be too late?

Subdued by fear and fatigue, Will turned into the drive to the pastel colored house he had restored with Robyn in Old Town, on the site of a ramshackle Conch cottage he had acquired several years ago. The fresh gravel crunched under the tires as the Classical Revival home came into view, the familiar lines of its historic Bahama shutters, gingerbread detail and hipped roof outlined dark against the lightening sky. To the side was a separate garage, now in use as his combination workshop and office, a nautical brass lantern burning over the entrance. Behind the house lay a narrow stretch of rocks and the ocean.

Usually the sight of the house he and brother Vince had restored with their own two hands – the house whose special features and decoration he and Robyn had planned to ensure historical integrity and not without a few arguments – filled him with pride.

But not today. Today his stomach knotted and a sense of emptiness filled him. *God, let Robyn be all right. Let her be all right.*

Grimly he stopped the car in front of the garage. Vince woke up their father, and all four men got out.

Inside the house, it was worse. Everywhere Will looked, he was reminded of Robyn. The big overstuffed sofa she had placed in front of the HARC-approved French doors looking out over the ocean where the Atlantic and Gulf of Mexico meet. The yellow and aqua tablecloth covering the picnic table serving temporarily as their dining room table. The pink and gray granite topped island in the kitchen she had insisted she couldn't live without. The watercolors of the Latitudes beachfront on Sunset Key she'd hung in the entranceway despite his objection that the ocean all around them was all they needed.

For a second, he shut his eyes against the pain. Then, steeling himself, he opened his eyes and directed Raul to the guest room. It had only a single bed, but it was the best he could offer. His father could take the pull out sofa in his office, and Vince would have to bunk with him. The extra bedrooms did not have beds in them yet.

"I'm getting out of these damp clothes." Vince yanked the bow tie from his neck. "I'll borrow a pair of your jeans and we can both wait up for the police."

Trailed by Vince, Will headed for the master bedroom. With his hand on the clear glass antique doorknob, he hesitated. He knew without entering that Robyn's presence was strongest in the bedroom. Her clothes already hung in the walk-in closet; most of her makeup and toiletries lined the medicine chest in the ensuite bathroom. The antique sleigh bed she'd found at one of Susie's Estate Sales was made up with luxurious 600 count Egyptian cotton sheets and the crisp white and blue quilt she'd convinced him were well worth their price.

He opened the door and flicked on the light. A cleaning service had come in yesterday after he left to prepare the place for their return later that night, so everything was clean, polished, and ready for the honeymoon to begin. They'd planned to spend the night together in their home, and then leave this morning for Little Palm Island for a very special honeymoon.

His throat tightened when he caught sight of the resplendent Stargazer lilies on the pine dresser – the same kind of lilies that Robyn had carried down the aisle. He grimaced when he saw the turned-back sheets, the plumped up pillows, the note –

The note?

He sprang across the room and reached for it. Then he froze.

The three-line note was written in the same typeface, and on the same plain white multipurpose paper as the note the kidnappers had left behind the tent.

His throat dry, he started to read.

≈≈≈

The first hint that something was wrong occurred when Robyn tried to open her eyes.

She couldn't.

Or more correctly, when she opened them, all she saw was darkness. Her eyelashes fluttered against something soft, dark and impenetrable.

The second clue came when she tried to raise her hands to push aside whatever covered her eyes. She couldn't do that either. Something prevented her from raising her hands more than a few inches past her waist. Not only from raising them, but also from separating them more than a hand's width.

She pulled against the restraint, and felt the cut of metal on her wrists. Oddly enough, she heard nothing, not the clink of metal against metal, the whoosh of rope, not even the shifting or creaking of the padded surface on which she lay.

Confused, she lay back. She tried to focus on what she'd just discovered, but her groggy mind wouldn't allow it. It seemed as if she'd been drifting in and out of sleep for hours, ever since the reception . . .

The reception?

The thought jarred her and she groped her way through her disjointed thoughts. Whatever it was, she knew it was important, knew it had something to do with what was happening now.

Slowly the pieces started to fall into place. Will. Saint Mary's. The wedding. *Her* wedding to Will. Walking down the aisle with Raul. The reception on the beach. And then . . .

She concentrated, struggling to banish the disoriented, woozy feeling that had her in its grip. She'd left the reception to meet someone. Laura. Laura hadn't been dressed for the wedding, even though she had been invited.

A blurry image of the tent wobbling and starting to go down filled her head. No matter how hard she tried, she couldn't remember anything else.

And now she was here, tied up and blindfolded, her mouth dry, her lips cracked. But where was here? And why?

The first bubbles of panic started to surface, along with fear, but she fought them down. Panic never helped anyone, ever.

Taking deep breaths as she taught her students in her yoga classes, she forced herself to explore her situation. In her woozy condition, it was slow, painstaking work. Her wrists were cuffed, the cuffs tied with nylon cord to more of the same cord wrapped around her waist, and tied at her back, she guessed from the knot pressing into her. A blindfold wrapped around her head, held in place top and bottom with what felt like duct tape, tape that covered her ears and wrapped around the back of her head. Her right upper arm felt swollen and painful, much the way it had after her last flu shot.

She cleared her throat. It was sore and scratchy, but what she noticed most was the way the sound bounced around in her head. That, and the strange silence. She could hear nothing, not even the creak of the bed she assumed she lay upon. Were her ears plugged in some fashion?

And what was she wearing? Clearly not her wedding dress. She wriggled her toes. Her feet and legs were bare, though not in the least bit cold. In fact, the room or wherever she was lying was overly warm and smelled of dust and must. She still wore her strapless bra and the lacy thong she'd put on before the wedding, but over it all lay something that felt like a long t-shirt or nightgown. Whatever it was fell to mid-thigh.

She rolled to her side, then struggled to sit up. The bad news was that everything she couldn't see seemed to be spinning around her. The good news was that while she was tied up, she didn't appear to be tied *to* anything.

She lowered her head to her thighs, almost losing her balance in the process, and touched the blindfold. It was a piece of fleece, perhaps a headband secured in place with tape. If she could manage to lift the tape, she might be able to –

The blow hit her hard in the forehead, knocking her back onto the bed. Despite the earplugs and the duct tape, she could hear a faint voice or voices. It sounded as if they were arguing, though she could not make out the words.

A moment later she was yanked to a sitting position. Gloved hands removed the cuffs and wrenched her arms behind her back. She felt, rather than heard, the cuffs replaced on her wrists and secured to the rope at her waist. Then she was shoved onto her stomach, her face pressed to the musty mattress.

Once more she heard the higher voice. Then nothing.

She lay still for several minutes, afraid to move. Was she alone? There was only one way to find out.

She rolled to her side and cleared her throat. "Water," she croaked, her dry throat and mouth refusing to produce their usual sounds. "Please . . . I need water."

Nothing. Was she alone again? Now that she'd made the request for water, she realized how thirsty she was. She had no idea what time it was or when she had last drunk anything. Her tongue seemed to have grown in thickness and fuzziness, and the inside of her mouth tasted like old, filthy socks. God, there had to be someone around willing to give her some water.

The kidnapper flipped her over and, supporting her back with a gloved hand, sat her upright. Something plastic nudged her lips apart, and her head was yanked back by the hair. Water began to pour into her mouth, some of it finding her throat, the rest dribbling onto her chin and neck. She drank as fast as she could, almost choking in the process.

Just as abruptly, the bottle was removed. The mattress shifted and Robyn assumed the person had gotten up from the bed. She needed to act quickly, before whoever it was left.

"Please . . . I need to go to the washroom. I can't wait."

No response, but a moment later what she thought were the same gloved hands helped her to her feet. She was guided across a dusty floor – the grit stuck to her bare feet – and into another room. She knew it was another room, because her shoulder rubbed the doorframe. Something brushed her wrists, and suddenly they were free. A gloved hand took one of hers, and pulled her forward until her shin banged the cold hard surface of the toilet.

The kidnapper lowered her hand to the toilet seat, then released her, brushing against her as he rose. A vaguely familiar, not unpleasant scent reached Robyn, but the scent receded with her captor before she could identify it. Was he giving her privacy? She hoped so. She concentrated all her effort on finding her way around the small bathroom. When she was through, she stood up.

"I'm done now," she said loudly. Several seconds passed and she repeated herself. "I'm done n–"

Someone grabbed her wrist and jerked her forward. There was that faint scent again, its identity still elusive. A moment later her arms were yanked behind her back and the cuffs snapped back on. She was prodded across the floor until she ran into the bed frame and toppled onto the mattress. It struck Robyn that her captor must be slightly shorter than she was. The man's shoulder jabbed into her upper arm at least once.

22

With her hands cuffed behind her, lying on her back was uncomfortable, so she shifted onto her side, setting off a bout of dizziness. Was anyone still there? Was there any point in asking when she couldn't hear their answer anyway?

Suddenly she was overwhelmed by thoughts of Will. Where was he? How had this happened? He must be frantic by now, he and Vince, Mark and their father John. Would she ever see him again?

The last thought filled her with fear. Behind the blindfold, hot tears gathered in her eyes. They'd just got married. They were only getting started in what was supposed to be a long life together. How could this be happening?

And why was it happening to her?

CHAPTER THREE

"Wait? What do you mean, 'wait'? That's all you're going to do?"

The hefty middle-aged detective from the Monroe County Sheriff's Office whose name Will couldn't remember and the lanky, younger FBI Special Agent Jim Rolland exchanged a look. Rolland nodded and took the question.

"Mr. Ryder, we understand how upset you are. And no, we aren't going to wait. That's your job. We want you to stay here, close to the phone. Get some sleep, something to eat, but most of all, wait until the kidnappers contact you again. In the meantime, we'll be re-examining the crime scene and following leads, including where this note came from and how it got onto your bed when there are no signs of forced entry."

The note lay in the middle of the picnic table, slipped into a plain manila envelope, but Will didn't need to see it to know what it said: He'd memorized every word.

"*Be prepared to drop off the $1.5 million Tuesday morning in small denominations in a black sports equipment bag. Will contact you Monday night with details.*"

Along with the question of how the note got onto his bed, the words kept repeating in his head, like a mantra designed to inflict maximum anguish rather than the usual sense of peace. He'd always prided himself on his self-control, on his ability to stay calm and assess any situation in a rational manner. But now he wanted to lash out, physically and verbally, and it took the last of his frayed willpower to rein in his frustration. For Robyn's sake, for her safe return, he had to do it.

Clenching his fists under the tablecloth, he turned to his father-in-law. "Are you sure you can come up with the money? If not, my brothers, Dad and I –"

Raul waved his hands in disagreement. "No, no, no." He shook his head to emphasize the point. "I know how strapped – that's the correct word isn't it? – how strapped you are for money, yes?"

Will forced himself not to flinch at the reminder of his financial situation. He and Vince had poured every cent they had, and a lot of the bank's money too, into the house they'd restored for himself and Robyn. But the house, besides being their home, had also been built to showcase Ryder Brother's Construction skills and promote new business. And it had worked. They had signed a contract to restore one conch house, and were on the verge of finalizing two more contracts within the next few days.

He nodded. "True enough. But if you can't do it, I'll find a way." If he had to, he'd call on every bank, every friend and relative to help out. His father was asleep on the sofa in the office now, and Vince sat silent and brooding at the end of the table, but he knew without asking that they'd do the same.

Raul smiled sadly. "That's not necessary, Will. You know I am working on expanding the consulting side of my mining business to the States. Because of that, I have already negotiated a line of credit worth several millions.

To get the money for the ransom will take only a phone call."

"Thank you." The last person in the world Will wanted to take anything from was Raul. But this was different. This was Robyn. He'd swallow his pride – hell, he'd swallow the whole damn house and everything he owned – if it meant he'd get her back.

Raul drummed his fingers on the table. Will couldn't help noticing the difference between them. Though Raul was of medium build and only a few inches shorter, his hands were almost delicate, the fingers long and tapered and well manicured. In contrast, Will's hands, though clean enough, were rough and callused, with nicks and scars on several knuckles. The hands of a man who made his living through physical labor.

Raul frowned and looked at the two officers. "But I don't like it."

"Don't like what, Sir?" An edge of impatience in his voice, Special Agent Rolland spoke up before Will could.

"No." Raul shook his head. "It is not the money. It is this whole kidnapping. There is something very odd about it."

"Odd?" Rolland raised his sandy eyebrows.

"As you know, Leopoldo and De Guzman have had to deal with kidnappers in both Argentina and Colombia after they abducted members of our staff. In my experience, the kidnappers are willing and prepared to negotiate, usually settling for a lower ransom than originally demanded. They also usually provide evidence that the victim is still alive."

Raul paused, as if to make sure his words had sunk in. "But this time the kidnappers, whoever they are, have indicated no willingness to negotiate. They appear to have assumed that we will get the amount demanded without a problem. This means they are either extremely well-informed about Robyn and the people around her, or extremely inexperienced."

"Inexperienced?" Will asked.

"He's right." Special Agent Rolland nodded, in the first show of animation since he'd arrived on the scene. Though he couldn't have been much older than Will, his slightly stooped posture and gloomy expression made him look as if he remained under a perpetual dark cloud. "My gut reaction is that it's both. Someone who knows the family, but also someone who has never done this before."

Will grimaced. "That's fine, but what does it all mean? Does this improve our chances of getting Robyn back?"

Rolland and the other officer exchanged another of those glances that were starting to grate on Will's last nerve.

"Not necessarily." Rolland spoke slowly. "Inexperienced people do stupid things. That might play into our hands, improving our chances of catching them. But it also might be more dangerous for your wife. We have to be very careful."

The Monroe County detective weighed in. "We'll be interviewing the cleaning staff, as well as that woman who was knocked unconscious outside the tent. The techs will be here soon, looking for prints or anything else that might shed some light on who left the note."

"What about Ralph Kleiner?" For months Robyn's no-good ex-husband had been pestering her for handouts. They'd only been married for two short months following high school, but the scumbag had resurfaced when stories about the success of Robyn's fitness club had started showing up in the local *KONK Life* newspaper. The officers had duly noted his name when Will suggested him as a potential kidnapper, but hadn't mentioned him since.

"O.K. Kleiner, too. But we need to be careful. We don't want to panic the kidnapper into doing anything rash."

Anything rash? Will's stomach tightened. It didn't take a genius to know what that meant.

They had to be careful not to panic the kidnapper into killing Robyn.

≈≈≈

Robyn's shoulders and upper arms ached from the unnatural position tied behind her back, and she couldn't get comfortable on the flattened and misshapen mattress no matter which way she turned. Deprived of sight and sound and all indication of the passage of time, she had little idea how long she'd been held captive.

The only thing she knew for certain was that she'd been fed three times. Once a lumpy serving of oatmeal, another time tinned, lukewarm vegetable soup, and the last time, a processed cheese slice between two pieces of soft white tasteless bread. She could still smell the blobs of oatmeal and soup that had spilled onto the upper part of her clothing, and remained there, dried reminders of her meals. And the person who had fed her, in common with the one who gave her water or took her to the washroom, wore gloves. Sometimes leather, sometimes latex.

She suspected that someone was in the room with her, watching, all the time. But whoever was there didn't answer her questions – not that she could have heard the answers anyway – or always respond to her requests for water or to relieve herself. As time inched by, she came to the conclusion there were two different people. It was part intuition, part scent. The person who'd been there first, the one who'd fed her the oatmeal and appeared to be shorter than she was, exuded a faint scent she thought she recognized, but which she still couldn't identify. The second person smelled vaguely of alcohol, and handled her more roughly than the first.

And then there was the panic. Panic and fear, swirling just below the surface of her control. Every once in a while the eddies intensified until she could barely breathe. Her heart palpitated wildly and she broke out in a sweat. She had to work harder than she'd ever worked in her life to keep from hyperventilating or screaming in terror, to keep the sense of helplessness from overwhelming her and leaving her a quivering, sobbing victim.

At the very worst of times, only her belief in Will saved her. After her first short and violent marriage, she'd had trouble trusting any man. She'd been scared. But with Will it had been different. His good nature and honesty had been like a ray of sunshine in a life experience made cautious and cynical. She was sorry now she'd dithered so much about getting married again. She knew Will was out there now, looking for her, doing everything he could to get her back. The thought of his strong arms around her gave her strength.

Suddenly an arm snaked under her neck and she was yanked upright. A cloth was jammed into her mouth. The next moment she was dragged to her feet and shoved along the dusty floor.

A rush of cool, fresh air told her they had come outside. Was it night? She sniffed the air, then stumbled down what she assumed was a set of two or three steps. Only the person grasping the cuffs kept her from falling.

Pushed and prodded from behind, she traversed a rough terrain. Gravel and tangles of heavy brush stung the soles of her bare feet. The toes of her right foot stubbed into something hard; the gag muffled her yelp of pain. Was that the faint turpentine smell from Brazilian pepper trees she smelled?

Without warning her feet were lifted out from under her. She felt herself being lowered, then dropped onto a hard, cold surface, probably metal or fiberglass. A second later something rough and scratchy was drawn over her legs and abdomen. Fresh air was replaced by the odor of must mixed with fishy tarp.

She felt a jerk or a tug, and then a distinct rocking motion that chilled her to the bone. She was in a boat. What in God's name was going to happen to her now?

≈≈≈

"You come alone. No weapons. No police. Only the money. You've got no more than a half hour."

The harsh voice of the kidnapper crackled across the line. Will's knuckles turned white on the receiver. "What about Robyn? Where will −"

The line went dead before Will could complete his question. He looked at Vince and Raul, Special Agent

Rolland and Jamieson, the detective from the sheriff's department. The retort of the phone at 4:07 a.m. had awakened them all from a restless sleep.

"Could you trace it?" Will asked.

Jamieson shook his head. "Not long enough. The guy's using a disposable cell."

"*Mierda!*"

Will grimaced. Raul spoke for them all. After the call Monday night ordering him to gas up the truck, he'd been prepared for a long drive this morning.

But the kidnapping had taken an unexpected turn. The caller –- a different voice from the one last night -- directed him to drive his fishing boat docked at Garrison Bight to the other side of the closer of the two islands visible from Mallory Square.

Will yanked a sweatshirt over his head and grabbed the black sports bag packed with the money from Raul. He patted the pocket of his jeans. Yeah, his utility knife was there.

"I'll alert the Sheriff's Office. They'll send boats this way," Rolland said.

Will whirled back to face him. "Tell them to keep their distance, okay? You heard the kidnapper. He said no police."

Rolland looked towards the ocean. "Can you get there in under thirty minutes? There might be a strong current through Fleming Cut."

"I'll get there."

Will headed out the front door and jumped on his blue Yamaha Zuma two-stroke scooter. He tossed the sports bag onto the floorboard of the scooter and raced up

Truman Avenue toward the Bight. His 23-foot Grady White 'Wishful Thinking' with a Yamaha F250 HP engine sputtered then roared to life. Thank God he kept the gas tank full and the engines in good repair.

Sitting at the helm, he headed out of the harbor, under the Palm Avenue bridge, past Houseboat Row into the waves towards the dark profile of the Fleming Cut Bridge towards Wisteria Island. The sun had yet to rise, but a thin band of gray light under a bank of clouds gathered over the city of Key West behind him. Will's eyes adjusted to the darkness, and he pushed the boat at full speed across the water ignoring the speed markers but making sure to stay in the channel so he didn't run aground. The crash of the bow hitting the water again and again echoed his heartbeat. Please, he prayed silently, please let me make it in time. Please.

As he tried to steer a wide berth around the liveaboards anchored in front of the island, the first glimmer of red appeared at the horizon. Narrowing his eyes, he surveyed the shoreline but could see nothing. In the 21-acre tangle of Australian Pine and the overgrown Brazilian Pepper Trees and shrubs was a derelict sailboat washed ashore and abandoned after Hurricane Wilma. He and Robyn had planned to investigate it sometime this summer. His throat tightened. Would they ever do it now?

He blasted around the corner and drove parallel to the shoreline. There was no obvious place to pull up a boat. But the kidnapper hadn't said anything about going on shore – just to meet him behind the island.

And then he saw it – a glint of light off something farther out in the water. Slowing, he squinted.

His heart leapt into his throat. It was a boat.

Slowing the engine further, he turned into the waves and made for the boat. The water bled crimson as the sun burst over the horizon. Will had to shield his eyes with one hand, and even then could barely see.

He killed the engine a few feet from the boat. It was a black fiberglass inboard, and a lone figure sat in the bow. When he came alongside, he noted the man was dressed in black, and wore a black hood and balaclava over his face. He held a rifle, the barrel pointed at Will. There didn't seem to be anyone else in the boat, only a dark tarp spread across the bottom behind the front row of seats.

Will swallowed his disappointment and tightened his grip on the throttle.

The second the engine noise died off, the man addressed him. The low snarl rang no bells for Will. "Throw the money into my boat."

For a second, Will considered heaving the bag into his face, and then jumping him. But his utility knife was no match for what looked like an assault rifle. And if Robyn wasn't there, what good would that do?

Carefully, he lifted the bag and tossed it into the other boat, about a yard away. One hand still on his rifle, the masked man unzipped the bag, glanced at the contents, then pulled back the zipper. He settled the bag on the floor beside the driver's seat then used the barrel of the rifle to shove Will's boat farther away.

"Where's my wife?" Will stood up. "I've kept my part of the bargain. Where is she?"

The man laughed, an unpleasant sound that turned Will's blood to ice. The man set down the rifle and moved to the stern. He fiddled with the tarp, tugging at something, then rose to his knees, a blanket-covered bundle in his arms. Without warning, he tossed it over the stern and returned to the driver's seat. He revved the motor and glanced at Will.

"You want your wife, you'd better get her before she drowns."

In a spray of foam and a roar of the engine he took off for open water.

CHAPTER FOUR

The shock of falling blind gave way to sheer terror when Robyn plunged beneath the surface of the water. She tried to use her arms to propel herself upwards, but they were bound behind her back. Kicking frantically, she raised her head out of the water, struggled free of the tarp, and maneuvered onto her back.

Without warning, a wave slapped over her face and she breathed in water. She managed to blow it out her nose, but it brought home her plight with a gruesomeness little else could.

She couldn't see or hear. Her mouth was gagged, her hands bound. She was alone and helpless, at the mercy of the waves in a black, silent world. Was this it? Was her life going to end here in the warm salty water, far from everyone she loved?

Another wave rolled over her head. She choked and struggled for air. How long could she hang on? How –

Something bumped against her. The gag muffled her scream. Something moved against her throat – an arm? It seemed as if something was supporting her too.

Unless this was the beginning of the end and she was hallucinating about being saved.

≈≈≈

Robyn! The flash of pale skin disappearing into the water jolted Will into action even before the masked man issued his departing taunt.

Focused on the spot where she had gone under, he grabbed the life ring on the boat, dropped the boarding ladder, kicked off his flip-flops, and leapt over the stern.

When he surfaced in the water, he saw a movement twenty feet ahead of him – a splash? In the choppy waves, it was hard to tell. He struck out for the splash, only to see another, and another. Then two long pale legs.

His eyes widened in horror when he saw the gag and duct tape and blindfold. Then he heard the labored attempt to expel ingested water.

He slipped one arm under her shoulders, another under her chin. "It's all right, baby," he crooned. "I'm here now. No one's going to hurt you."

To his relief, she didn't fight him the way panicked swimmers often fought their rescuers. Slowly he towed her back to the boat. It was only when he tried to draw her hands to the side of the boat that he realized her wrists were bound behind her.

Under his breath he swore. *Whoever had hurt her like this was going to pay.* He considered hauling himself into the boat first, and then her up after, but rejected it. He didn't want to leave her alone in the water a second longer than necessary.

After a moment to consider his options, he managed to lift her over his head and roll her over onto the swim platform. He winced at the thump of her body hitting the decking. He tossed his life jacket onto the deck then breathing heavily, heaved himself on board over the gunwale.

She lay on her side, unmoving. He gently pulled at the duct tape then his fingers attacked the knot of the cloth used to gag her. After several fumbles he undid it, pulled her up from the swim platform onto the deck, and pulled the gag free of her mouth.

"Robyn! Are you okay? Robyn?"

Fear squeezed his chest when she didn't respond. She was breathing; why wasn't she answering? What was wrong?

With shaking fingers he worked at the duct tape securing the blindfold. He ripped it away as carefully as he could, then pushed the sodden band off her head. Her eyes remained closed, wedding makeup smeared across her lids and under her eyes.

"Robyn, please." Gently he kissed her eyelids, one after the other, praying that she was all right. She had to be all right. Lifting her into his arms, he kissed her cheeks and her lips.

After a moment her eyes fluttered open, then quickly shut again, as if the dim light were painful. She tried again, managing to keep her eyes open a slit.

"Will?"

His name was a croak, but it was the most beautiful sound he'd ever heard. His breath caught. With difficulty he responded. "Yes. It's me."

She coughed and turned her head. Something small and red fell to the floor. He stared at it for a moment before realizing what it was – an earplug. He brushed the hair away from her other ear. The end of another earplug was just visible. He plucked it out and threw it overboard, then gathered her closer.

"Oh, sweetheart. Everything's going to be fine now. Just fine."

≈ ≈ ≈

Seventeen hours later

"Come to bed, Will."

Robyn's lips parted in the smile that had roped Will in from the first moment he'd seen her more than two years ago, leading a combination Tai Chi and Yoga class at Island Fit. Izzie, the manager, had invited him there to talk about renovations, but all he'd seen was Robyn, her wavy golden-brown hair in a ponytail, her smile infectious as she encouraged the participants to try ever more challenging poses. It was a good thing Robyn was scrupulously honest, because he would have agreed to any price, no matter how lowball, just to be able to work near her.

But now it was important to resist. Robyn's wellbeing depended on it. He shook his head. "No. You go ahead. You need to rest."

She did need rest. She may have dozed once or twice in the hours since Will had pulled her from the water, but for the most part she had been awake. At the Lower Keys Medical Center on Stock Island, attached to Key West via the Cow Key bridge, they had checked her over thoroughly, including blood and urine tests to try to determine how she was drugged. Followed by hours with the police, where she told them everything she could remember of her kidnapping and the more than fifty hours of captivity. With her eyes covered and her ears plugged, it wasn't much, except that the place where she had been hidden smelled musty and dusty, and was located near what smelled like Brazilian Pepper trees.

And then there were the demands of family and friends and co-workers. Vince, their father, Raul, her late mother's partner George McMaster, all wanted to know everything about her captivity, as well as what had transpired out on the water between the kidnapper and Will. Izzie had paced the hospital's hallways, waiting for the first chance to throw herself at Robyn, while friends and staff gathered in the waiting room. Robyn, for her part, had been incensed at the amount of the ransom. Over Raul's objections, she hotly promised she would get it back to him, whether or not the kidnapper was ever found.

That was up to the Sheriff's Office and the FBI. They had inserted a transmitter in the sports bag holding the ransom, but it had stopped transmitting minutes after the kidnapper sped off in his boat. Though Will had called on his cell the moment he was sure Robyn was okay, police boats didn't arrive until well after they returned to Garrison Bight.

Robyn tugged on his hand now, with some of the same insistence. "And you don't need rest too? Knowing you, you didn't sleep or eat any more than I did in the last three days. Maybe less."

She paused. "Besides, I don't want to be alone."

Will raised one eyebrow. "I thought you couldn't wait for everyone to leave." Vince and his father had left a couple of hours earlier, and Raul and George only ten minutes ago. Despite himself, Will had developed new respect for his father-in-law. The man had hung in through every minute of their ordeal, his ideas, his support – hell, his money! – invaluable. More than anyone, Raul was responsible for Robyn's safe return, and Will would never forget it. He'd join Robyn in paying back the ransom if it took the rest of his life.

But finally they'd gotten rid of everyone, with the exception of the lone sheriff's deputy cooling his heels in the foyer. The Sheriff's Office had offered protection until the locks had been changed and a new security system installed tomorrow, and they had accepted.

"I didn't mean *you*, Will." A hint of mischief flickered in the dark brown eyes so like her father's, but it didn't relieve the exhaustion visible on her gaunt pale face, or lighten the dark smudges under her eyes. The small, curved scar on her left cheek, a gift from the fist of her first husband, was stark against flesh white and puckered from three days under duct tape. Her next words confirmed her weariness.

"I do want to sleep – desperately. But I want you right beside me. I want your arms around me." Her voice rose. "Think you can do that?"

He reached for her other hand and raised them both to his lips. "I insist on it."

Slipping one arm around her waist, he guided her to the bedroom, sat her on the edge of the bed, and dropped to his knees. He removed the gray wool socks from her feet, then cupped the heel of her left foot in his hand and raised it. Gently, but firmly, he ran his hands along the sides of her foot and slid his palm under her arch. He massaged each perfectly shaped toe, kissed the top of her foot then reached for the other.

With a giggle, she pulled it out of his reach. "What *are* you doing?"

He grinned. "I'm checking you out. Every part of you. Making sure the kidnappers didn't make off with a toe or a finger or anything else."

Her laughter, the first since her return, was the most beautiful sound in the world. "You'd better do it fast then. At the rate you're going, I'll be asleep before you've made it to my knees."

"Not if I have anything to do with it." He nipped her perfectly manicured big toe, and was rewarded with another smile that beamed its way right into his heart.

Gently he pushed her back until she was lying on the bed. He undid her jeans, and pulled them over her hips and down her legs. Starting at her ankles, he slowly ran the rough pads of his thumbs up the insides of her calves, her knees, and her thighs, stopping just below her panty line. She smelled of soap and clean denim and everything warm and feminine. He paused, his palms warm on her cool skin.

She shivered. When she spoke, her voice was huskier than it had been only a moment before. "Everything fine there?"

"As far as I can tell," he said, not missing a beat. "But I won't know for sure until I've seen all of you."

"Really?" She paused. "Then what are you waiting for?"

With a chuckle, he lifted her farther onto the bed, then sat beside her. He undid the buttons on her long-sleeved cotton blouse then eased her out of it. His gut twisted when he saw the wrists rubbed raw by the metal cuffs, the ugly green and purple bruises blossoming along her arms and shoulders. He touched each bruise with his fingertips, trailed them along the raw skin.

Anger exploded inside him. Who could have done this? Why? Was it all for money? Somehow he managed to choke it down. He looked up at her. "Does it hurt?"

"Yes."

The simple admission awed him. It was one more reason why he loved her. No dramatics, no play-acting, just the truth. That was his Robyn. It was up to him to make sure no one ever hurt her again.

"But you know what hurts the most?"

He jerked away from her. "They did something else to you?"

She grabbed his hand and pulled it down to her flat belly. "It's not what you're thinking. Nothing physical."

"What?"

She held his hand still until he quieted, her calm seeping into him. He looked at her. The love and the warmth in the depths of her brown eyes sparked a familiar yearning and hunger inside him. He wanted her so much.

"They took our wedding night away. Our first night together as husband and wife. I was looking forward to it so much. And I thought about it again and again while I was kidnapped. I missed you so much."

"Oh, baby." He gathered her into his arms, and kissed her forehead. "We'll have plenty of other nights. And mornings, and afternoons. . . "

"I know." Her eyes glistened with unshed tears. She smiled crookedly and hooked one finger over the neck of his t-shirt until they were nose to nose.

"But I don't want to wait any longer. Do you?"

For a long moment he held her gaze. Need pooled in her coffee-colored eyes, and vibrated from her heated skin, the same need curling in his belly and flickering through his veins. Despite fatigue, despite common sense, despite bruises and cuts, there was no denying what they both wanted.

Slowly, deliberately, he lowered his lips to hers. Let the wedding night begin.

≈≈≈

One instant Robyn was asleep, the next wide-awake. She lay still and alert in the darkness, trying to pinpoint her position.

Bit by bit her senses filled in the picture and she relaxed. Will's solid warmth had her back, while his arm curved protectively around her waist. Beneath her rustled the expensive cotton sheets she had chosen for their bed. His warm breath tickled her ear. Beyond that, she could hear the crowing of roosters in the distance, getting ready to announce the dawn.

She snuggled deeper into Will's embrace. With him next to her, she felt safe, invincible. No one could get her here. Will wouldn't let them, and neither would she. They'd fight together to the death.

In the darkness, she smiled at her over-dramatization. Though she still ached all over, Will's tender lovemaking had gone a long way to erasing the horror of the past few days. He treated her like the most precious of treasures, delicately teasing her to the highest of heights, and asking nothing in return. She'd never felt so loved, so cherished, so secure. And ready now to give back what he'd given her a hundredfold.

Unable to go back to sleep, she slipped out from under his arm, and padded naked over to the ensuite bathroom. Quietly she shut the door behind her and flipped on the light. A crystal vase of fresh Stargazer lilies sat on the counter near the sink, their perfume filling the air. The aroma should have reminded her of their wedding day, but this morning it only made her gag. She opened the door to the hall and set them on the floor outside. As soon as she was dressed, they'd be in the yard waste bin.

Back in the bathroom, she pondered her morning after gift to Will. Where would it be? Back in bed, under the covers? Or in the double shower, hot water sluicing over their heated and soaped bodies? With a guard camped out in the foyer, anywhere else was out of the question, at least this morning.

Memories of another morning, another shower, filled her head, and she grinned. So this wasn't Island Fit, where they'd made love on the exercise equipment and showered in the women's changing room just minutes before the staff arrived to open for the day. Neither of them needed the chance of discovery to heighten their lovemaking. Just each other.

Smiling to herself, and ignoring the gaunt bruised woman reflected back at her from the shell-framed mirror, Robyn pulled out fresh, fluffy towels from the linen closet and hung them over the racks. She opened a drawer and took out a vanilla scented candle in a frosted holder, lit it, and set it on the quartz countertop. Between the dim lighting and the falling water from the rain showerhead, Will wouldn't even notice her bruises.

She paused. There was something missing. Special soap! That was it. She'd brought back a large box of fun assorted handcrafted soaps from the dreamy smelling shop 'Purely Paradise' on Duval. She'd given most of the soaps away, but kept a small quantity of her favorite shapes, a starfish and a palm tree. Will was willing to wash with them after work every day because she loved the smell of these island soaps on his hands and face. Each shape had its own fragrance. Soaping themselves everywhere with it would be even better.

She opened the cupboard under the sink and rummaged through the cleaning supplies and toiletries stored there. Where was it? She was sure she'd left the box under the sink. Surely they weren't out. Or had the cleaning ladies moved it?

She tried the linen closet next, checking each shelf, looking behind the towels they'd received as wedding presents, moving knickknacks and her less expensive sheet sets. Finally she could see the box, at the very back under the bottom shelf, on the floor. Moving another box out of the way, she pulled it out.

The corrugated cardboard carton had once held a dozen or so of the mixed soaps. She lifted the box and was surprised by how heavy it was. Had Will stuffed something else into it? The last time she'd looked, there were only two or three bars of the fun shapes left.

She put the box on the counter and undid the flaps. Three bars of soap sat right at the top.

But what was underneath?

She picked up the soaps and looked into the box. Her eyes widened and her stomach lurched.

Money.

The box was filled almost to the top with stacks and stacks of money. Clean, crisp bills that looked too new to be real, too pristine to have ever been in circulation.

A nasty doubt flashed into her head. Horrified, she tried to blot it out.

Behind her, the door swung open. Her gaze rose to the mirror. Will, his face attractively grizzled, his hair mussed, smiled at her. "Hey, what are you doing up so early?"

She tried to answer, but all she could think of was the money.

She saw his expression change in the mirror. "What's wrong? What have you got there?"

With shaking hands she lifted the box and turned to face him. She held it out to him.

He looked down. She knew at that moment he recognized what it was. His face turned a sickly gray. He cussed and jerked his gaze back to hers.

"Where did this come from?"

CHAPTER FIVE

Robyn didn't answer. Instead, she voiced the same unpalatable possibility that had occurred to Will.

"Is it . . . could it be some of the ransom money?"

Will swallowed. "I don't know," he said slowly. "It could be."

It was the last thing he wanted to believe, but there was no point denying the possibility – or the unavoidable conclusion that went along with it. If this was the ransom money, then the kidnappers not only had access to their home but also were people close to them. Friends. Employees. Relatives, even.

Robyn paled, and Will knew the same thoughts were going through her head. Hardly the welcome home he'd wanted for her. Last night had been wonderful, but the shadows of what had happened since the wedding hovered in the corners of the room. This morning he'd hoped to dispel those shadows for good, and restore his wife's delight in their new life together.

Clearly, that was not to be.

Carefully Robyn set the box on the bathroom's countertop.

"Where did you find it?" he asked.

"It was in the linen closet, behind some gift boxes." She paused. "You recognize the box, don't you? It's the one that held the soap I bought from Purely Paradise. I'm sure I left it under the sink. Unless the cleaning ladies moved it?"

Will shook his head at the unspoken hope in Robyn's question. "Maybe. But that still doesn't explain where the money came from."

He turned and started for the bedroom.

"Where are you going?"

He scooped up his jeans from the high back wicker chair where he'd tossed them last night. "The officer on guard. The police need to know about the money right away."

≈≈≈

It wasn't a look Will had ever seen on Robyn's face before, or one he ever wanted to see again. The frightened, deer-caught-in-the-headlights look lasted only a moment, but it was long enough to make him deeply uneasy.

Nor did he like the expression Special Agent Rolland had worn from the moment he'd walked through the door fifteen minutes earlier. Rolland's gloomy hound dog features had perked up as if he were on the trail of a particularly tasty prey. His questions only made it worse.

"This is definitely part of the ransom money. The serial numbers confirm it." Rolland nodded at the box sitting on the picnic table in the dining room in the middle of a pool of morning sunshine. Then, with a calculated casualness, he turned his head to Will. "Any idea how the money got into the box?"

"No." Robyn echoed Will's response. He smiled his gratitude at her support, but her eyes didn't quite meet his.

"Tell me again: Who has keys to this house?"

"Both of us. The cleaning ladies. My brother Vince." Will looked at Robyn again. "Have I missed anyone?"

50

Her gold-streaked hair, as yet uncombed, fanned out in waves around her face as she shook her head. "No."

"Do you know how much is in the box?" Rolland's eyes narrowed. He glanced at Robyn then looked at Will.

"No."

"Hmm." Rolland directed his attention to Robyn. "Where did you say you found the box again?"

"In the linen closet." Robyn's voice cracked. She cleared her throat and went on. "It was behind a couple of empty boxes that had held wedding presents."

"So you'd say it was hidden?"

Robyn bit her bottom lip, a sure sign of nervousness. "Yes. No. Maybe. I don't know. I'm sure the box was under the sink in the ensuite the last time I saw it. Though I suppose the cleaning ladies could have moved it."

"I'll be sure to ask them."

Rolland's tone grated on Will's nerves. Suddenly he figured out why; the FBI agent suspected him, if not of kidnapping, at least of trying to benefit financially from his wife's abduction.

Will clenched his fists. It had been a dozen years since the law had cast a suspicious eye on him or his brothers for the break-ins and petty crimes that had plagued the Meadows neighborhood of Key West where they'd lived with their father. But it was still hard not to rise to the bait, to respond to the unspoken accusations that had followed them wherever they'd gone, or at least until Vince had joined the local police force and Mark had become a lawyer.

Slowly Will unfurled his fists, using the time to leash in his temper. "Have you spoken to Laura yet?"

"Who?"

"Laura Rennick. You know, Robyn's employee. The one who was found knocked out behind the reception tent. How is she?"

"She's fine now. A few stitches and a mild concussion, but she'll be all right. She was released from the hospital Sunday morning."

Rolland glanced at Robyn. "You know she's quit her job?"

"What are you talking about?" Robyn frowned. "She's my best fitness instructor, best personal trainer too."

"Not any more. She told my guys she quit the day before the wedding."

"Quit? Why?"

"Apparently there was some unpleasantness about a client's wallet being found in the pocket of Miss Rennick's jacket that afternoon. Your manager – Izzie Sudak, isn't it? – agreed not to press charges if Rennick resigned on the spot. So she did."

Robyn's brow furrowed. She looked at Will. "D'you think that's why she didn't come to the wedding? And why she sent me the note asking to meet her by the bar?"

"That would –"

Rolland cut Will off. "She said she was too embarrassed to go to the wedding, but wanted to explain to you in person why she wasn't there."

"What about Robyn's kidnapping? Is she involved?" Will asked.

Rolland shook his head. "So far it looks like a coincidence that she was there at the same time Mrs. Ryder here was kidnapped. Rennick's car was in the parking lot. Her boyfriend was working. We've been watching her ever since she returned home, but she hasn't done anything to raise suspicion."

Will had met Laura on several occasions. He was glad she wasn't one of the kidnappers. But if not her, who? He pressed on. "What about the cleaning ladies? Have you –"

Abruptly Rolland stood up. "There's nothing to tell you yet." He addressed the tech who had just entered the room from the hallway. "Got everything you need?" The man nodded and headed to the table to collect the box of money.

"All right then." Rolland's lips twisted in a humorless smile. "Stay close, folks. We should have more for you tomorrow."

≈≈≈

The ransom money in the box and the visit from Special Agent Rolland had taken the shine off what should have been a wonderful day. The bright summer sun warmed Robyn's skin, a brisk, tropical breeze made the palm trees rustle, and best of all she was home, safe, with Will.

But now, in the middle of the morning, as she leaned against the railing of their porch overlooking the ocean nursing a cup of Cuban *'Cafe con Leche'*, she was weighed down with ugly thoughts and careening emotions. The feel of the yet-to-be-painted planks of the porch under her bare feet normally made her think of lazy days at home and at the beach. Now the same planks sparked memories of stumbling, bound and blindfolded not knowing where she was or what was going to happen next. Memories of fear and panic, ugly emotions that should never be a part of a loving home with Will.

Suddenly familiar, comforting arms wrapped around her. Will nuzzled her neck, his lips warm and gentle. He stroked her arms easing away the tension coursing through her. She leaned back into his embrace grateful for his reassuring presence and its ability to dispel at least some of her fears.

His grip tightened. "I love you," he murmured. "I'm so glad we got you back safely. I don't know what I would have done if anything had happened to you."

She savored his words, his touch, slowing moving her derriere against his groin and delighting in his growing response. Still, she couldn't quite blot out the worry. She set her coffee on the railing and turned to face him.

"How do you think that money got into our linen closet?" she asked.

Lines she hadn't noticed before tightened around his eyes and mouth. "I wish I knew," he said darkly. "I don't like it. Any of it. Between the ransom note left on our bed – and now this – it's getting creepy. Creepy because it means at least one of the kidnappers has had access to our house."

He paused. "And you know what that means?"

She was reluctant to put into words any of the doubts gnawing at her ever since she found the money in the closet, but she did it anyway. "That the kidnapper, or kidnappers, is someone one of us knows."

Will nodded.

Her fingers tightened on his arms. "Well, at least the guard is still here. When are the guys from Cardinal Security arriving?"

"Around three or four."

"Good. I'll –"

"You bastard!"

Before Will could turn around, Raul rushed through the French doors, his dark eyes blazing. The smaller man leapt on Will, grabbing him around the neck and throwing wild punches at his head, all the while letting go a stream of invectives in Spanish. It was like an angry bee attacking an unsuspecting bull.

"Raul! Stop it!" Robyn shouted. She stepped forward to intervene but Will defended himself, ramming his elbow into his father-in-law's gut.

The counterattack had the desired effect. Raul let go of Will, and doubled over clutching his stomach. He was clearly in pain, but not enough to stop him gasping out orders. "*Ladrón!* Get that thief, Sergei. Beat him into the ground!"

For the first time, Robyn noticed Sergei Kakovka, standing just inside the house behind the open French doors. The tall, fit Russian, a business colleague of her father's, made no move to follow the command. Instead, he stood back, his hands in the pockets of his lightweight gray suit, an amused expression on his broad, Slavic face, his full lips twisted into a ghost of a smile. For a second his gray eyes met Robyn's and he shrugged as if to say, "what can I do?"

It was a moot point. The moment Raul regained his breath he leapt at Will again, fists flailing. Will raised his arms to fend off the blows. "What's with you, Raul? Are you crazy?"

Robyn grabbed one of her father's arms and tried to tug him away from Will. A second later, Sergei joined her taking Raul's other arm. Between the two of them they yanked her father, struggling and kicking, to the far side of the porch.

Will lowered his arms and stood by the railing, tensed for another attack.

Raul tried to break away. Robyn dug her fingers into his arm. "Stop it. Have you lost your mind?"

Raul stopped his struggling and looked at her in disbelief. "Don't you know? He stole the ransom money! He endangered your life by taking some of the money meant for the kidnappers. He doesn't care about you. Only the money!"

Shock coursed through Robyn. "What? What are you talking about? Will didn't steal any money!"

"No?" Raul straightened. His dark eyes narrowed and bored into hers. "Then how did the ransom money get into your closet? How else could it have gotten there?"

Robyn looked at Will.

He frowned and shook his head. "Give it a rest, Raul. I know you don't like me – you've never liked me – but you know I wouldn't do anything to hurt Robyn."

Raul ignored him. "Don't you see?" he pleaded to Robyn. "He is not good enough for you. He has never been good enough for you. Get your things and come with me to my hotel. Leave this *hijo de puta* here to rot."

Son of a bitch? Robyn's throat tightened at her father's name-calling. In desperation, she looked at Will to inject some sanity into the conversation but found no help there. A muscle pulsed in his jaw; it looked as if he was using all his will power to keep from leaping across the porch and pounding out his accuser.

Over her father's head, Robyn met Sergei's gaze. The sympathy there was palpable, but he made no move to help her refute Raul's accusations either. She swallowed and girded herself to try again. "I don't know how you can say those things about Will. You've got no reason to think he took the money."

"No?" Raul sneered. "Ask your husband. Ask him about the two building contracts he just lost."

"I haven't lost any contracts." Will straightened. "Vince would have told me. Besides, what contracts I have or don't have are none of your business."

Raul tried to leap at Will again, only to be held back by Sergei and Robyn. "You're a thief. A no-good *ladrón* who is not good enough to be anywhere near my daughter!"

Robyn had never seen her father so angry, his polished manners thrown aside, his emotions laid bare. She'd known there was antagonism between Will and Raul – there'd been that argument just before the wedding -- but because they'd always been outwardly civil to each other, she'd let it lie, assuming it would work itself out with time. But to believe Will was a thief? That he'd taken some of the ransom money?

She tried to calm her father. "Raul, please. You're upset. Will would never –"

"He's a thief! He does not love you. He –"

"That's enough," Will snapped. "Get out. Now. You and Sergei. Both of you. I don't have to take this abuse in my own home. Get out."

"Your home?" The smaller man's lip curved in scorn. "The bank might have something to say about that."

"Raul, please!" Over her father's head, Robyn pleaded silently with Sergei to take him away. The Russian was much younger than Raul, probably in his mid thirties, but her father respected his opinion. Sergei nodded.

Will took a step forward. "Get out. Before I throw you out."

Ignoring Will, Raul shook free of Robyn's grasp. He took her hand. "Robyn, *mi querida hija*. Please come with me. I don't want to leave you here with this criminal. It's not safe."

Will interrupted. "She's fine. Now get out."

"Raul, please go. It's better that way. You don't have to worry about me. I'm okay."

Raul looked at Robyn. Slowly his gaze hardened, and he turned back to Will. To Robyn's amazement, he spat at his feet.

"I leave now. Only because my daughter wants me to leave. But do not think I am dropping this. You stole my money. You put my daughter's life in danger. Do not think you're going to get away with it."

He whirled about, Sergei still gripping his arm, and stomped off the porch, and back into the house. The front door slammed, the noise echoing through the house. A moment later, a car engine roared to life in the distance, then grew fainter as her father and Sergei tore out of the drive in Raul's rented Mercedes.

Robyn didn't move and neither did Will. The air between them bristled with tension, but Robyn couldn't think of anything to say. She was still grappling with the shock of Raul's startling accusations and his animosity towards Will.

Will broke the silence first. "You don't believe him, do you?" he demanded.

Robyn hesitated a moment too long. "No, I –"

"Oh, great." Will stalked to the railing, picked up her abandoned coffee mug, and heaved it out onto the patio stones below. He turned and faced her, his hands grasping the railing on either side of him. "How can you think I'd steal your father's money? Especially the money meant to ransom you?"

"It's not that."

"Then what is it?" Anger flared in Will's eyes, then dimmed. He turned away, towards the water. When he spoke again, his voice had a thick, strangled quality she'd never heard before.

"Do you have any idea what it was like after you were kidnapped? How it felt to wait for hours, and days, waiting for the kidnappers to make contact, not knowing whether you were dead or alive? Do you?"

"I –"

Robyn gave up on words. She went to him, wrapped her arms around his waist and leaned against his back. Through his thin t-shirt she could hear the angry pounding of his heart.

"I don't think you stole the money," she said quietly. "But I can imagine why it looks that way to Raul. It *was* really freaky to find the money in our home. If I didn't know you so well, I might think the same thing, especially after the way Agent Rolland questioned you and me. But I know you, and I know you'd never do anything like that."

In answer, Will covered her hands with his. A minute passed, then another. Finally he removed her arms and turned to face her. He pulled her against him, his hands at her hips. The tension faded from his face and his eyes met hers. "Good. Because what you think means more to me than anything else."

He lowered his mouth to hers and kissed her, gently at first, then with increasing passion. His kiss ignited her own hunger, and she responded with fervor, trying to blot out the uneasiness spawned by the morning's events. But when Will slid the straps of her camisole off her shoulders, she eased away.

She pulled his hands to her lips, kissed them then raised her head. "How do you think my father knew about the money? Agent Rolland left here less than an hour ago."

Will shrugged. "The ransom came from Raul's line of credit. Rolland must have called to let him know they'd recovered some of the money."

He frowned. "That reminds me. About something else your father said."

He stepped around her, crossed the porch and went inside. "I need to make one quick phone call." He turned his head and smiled at her. The naked heat in his eyes set off an answering sizzle in her. Her pulse quickened. "Then maybe we can retire to the bedroom for more of our marital duties."

He grabbed the portable phone off the table, punched in a number and paced towards the kitchen. Whoever he called answered. Robyn could hear Will's voice, but was too far away to make out the words. Pulling up her camisole straps, she crossed the porch and entered the house.

Will whirled around, his face white. "What?"

The alarm in that one word sent a chill down Robyn's back. With growing tension, she watched as Will listened, his expression becoming grimmer by the second, his responses short and terse. Finally, with a curt "all right", he jabbed the off button and lowered the phone to the silver cradle.

He looked at her. "You won't believe this, but your father was right."

"Right?" Robyn frowned. "Right about what?"

"About the contracts. Raul was right. We lost the contracts to restore those two houses the day before the wedding."

CHAPTER SIX

The next morning, persistent pounding, interspersed with the ringing of the doorbell, woke Robyn from the doze she'd fallen into after the alarm buzzed at five forty-five a.m. Will shot out of the bathroom, bare-chested and wiping shaving cream from his jaw. Muttering, he grabbed a Ryder Brother's Construction logoed white t-shirt from the dresser and pulled it over his head.

Robyn sat up. Between worrying about the money and the lost contracts and what it all meant, she hadn't slept well last night. She glanced at the clock. "Who'd be at the door now? It's only six fifteen."

"Whoever it is, it must be important. Unless it's Vince thinking he's funny." Will headed for the door.

As the bedroom door shut behind him, Robyn threw back the sheets and jumped out of bed. She slipped into a silk kimono style robe, and padded for the door, belting it around her as she went. She wanted to know who it was too. If it was Vince, he was getting a piece of her mind.

"Hey, Vince, you –"

Robyn lurched to a halt, her hands frozen on the wide silk sash. The foyer was full of men, some of them in the hunter green uniform of the Monroe County Sheriff's Office, none of them Vince. In the middle of it all stood Will, his face and chest against the wall, his wrists handcuffed behind his back.

"What's going on? What are you doing to my husband?" Robyn demanded.

The blur of faces and bodies focused into one she recognized. Special Agent Rolland, one of only two men in suits, cleared his throat and looked at her, his long face impassive. "Your husband is under arrest –"

"What for?"

" . . . For your kidnapping, ma'am," the agent continued as if she hadn't interrupted.

Frustration and anger erupted in Robyn. "That's impossible. How could he have kidnapped me? He was at the wedding or here at the house with you or family the whole time."

Rolland's phlegmatic expression didn't change. "He may not have been the one to seize you at the reception, but we have reason to believe he set the whole thing up and stood to benefit from it."

A horrible thought crossed Robyn's mind. "It's the money, isn't it? The money we found here yesterday?"

"I'm not at liberty to discuss the evidence or the reasons for your husband's arrest." Rolland opened his suit jacket, and removed a folded paper. "We've got a warrant to search the house, and to take the printer and computer for testing. His truck, too."

He turned to one of the sheriff's deputies. "Take Ryder out to the car."

Robyn rushed forward. "No, you can't –"

Will shook his head. "It'll be all right, Robyn. Just let Mark know as it looks like I'll be needing a lawyer."

The deputy moved to grab Will's arm, but Will jerked out of reach. He nodded to his bare feet. "I need shoes."

Rolland raised a hand in assent. "Let him get his shoes."

Like an automaton, Robyn slid open the closet and took out Will's scuffed work boots. She put them on the floor. "He needs socks, too."

Before anyone could stop her, she scurried for the bedroom. Suddenly clammy and nauseous, she pulled open drawer after drawer until she found Will's underwear and sock drawer. She grabbed the first pair of work socks she found, stood up quickly then had to grab the dresser for support as a wave of nausea swept over her.

She swallowed and forced the sick feeling down. She was no good to Will with her head in the toilet. Satisfied she wouldn't throw up all over the foyer, she returned to the entranceway.

Rolland reached for the socks, but she batted his hand away. "I can do it."

She knelt at Will's feet. Awkwardly, she pulled one sock on, then the other. By the time Will had shoved his feet into his boots, and she started to lace them up, she was fighting back tears.

"Leave it, Robyn," Will said quietly. "What I need you to do is call Mark. Tell him what's happened."

Shakily, Robyn rose to her feet and looked at Will. She swallowed hard. How could this be happening? She'd loved Will almost from their first moments together, but experience had made her cautious. It had taken far longer for her to trust him – and now this?

What if she was wrong? As wrong as she'd been about the first man she'd married? She blanched. The treacherous thought appalled her, but she couldn't take it back. The damage was done; the first seed of serious doubt planted.

Misinterpreting her expression, Will smiled reassuringly. "It'll be all right. I mean it. Just call Mark. He'll know what to do. Call my Dad too."

His eyes crinkled at the edges and one side of his mouth dropped in the crooked grin she had always loved. A patch of dark stubble on the left side of his jaw testified to the fact the police had arrived in the middle of his shaving.

Squelching the horrid doubt, she reached up and touched his jaw, the stubble prickly under her fingers. She tried to smile, but couldn't quite manage it. "You missed a spot."

Her fingers slipped over to his mouth, and he kissed the tips, his gaze meeting hers. "I love you, Robyn. Don't worry. This will be cleared up soon."

Then the deputy hustled him out the door to the waiting car.

≈≈≈

The moment the door shut, Robyn scrambled to the kitchen for her cell phone. Cursing her shakiness, she scrolled to the Ms to find Mark's number. He was twenty-eight, the same age as she was, and had been practicing criminal law in Key West for the past three years. As she called his number, a man in the brown uniform of the sheriff's department entered the room.

To Robyn's relief, Mark picked up on the second ring. "Morn–"

"It's Will. He's been arrested," she yelped into the receiver before Mark could complete his greeting. "The FBI is taking him away now."

"What? Is this Robyn? Hang on a second."

In the background she could hear water running and the babble of a radio or TV announcer, then nothing. She glared at the pudgy-faced sheriff's deputy as he settled against the kitchen counter to watch her.

After what seemed like minutes but couldn't have been more than thirty seconds, Mark called her back. "Now slow down and tell me. What's going on?"

"The FBI and sheriff's deputies are here right now searching the house. They've just arrested Will for kidnapping me."

The dead silence echoed her own shock. "They've arrested Will for kidnapping you?" Mark finally asked, his tone incredulous. "Is that what you said?"

"Yes."

"Have you got any idea why?"

"It's got to be the money we found in the linen closet yesterday."

"What money?"

Robyn's fingers tightened on her Smartphone. "Will didn't tell you? I found some of the ransom money hidden in a box in the closet yesterday morning. We turned it over to the police as soon as we found it."

Mark cussed. If she'd had any doubts about the seriousness of what they'd found, his reaction erased them. "Anything else you should tell me?"

"Only that they're taking Will's computer, printer and his truck, too."

"Okay." Mark paused, and Robyn could almost feel his mind at work. "I've got a couple of things to take care of at the courthouse this morning, but I'll get on this right away. With any luck, we'll have him out on bail by tomorrow."

"Tomorrow?" Robyn's heart sank. "That long?"

"Are you all right?" Mark's concern almost broke her shaky control. She was glad when he barreled on removing the need for her to speak. "Because if you're not, I can send Sam over. She's here now and doesn't go to work until noon."

Sam was sweet, a hard-working juvenile probation officer. She was also Mark's girlfriend. But Robyn was too distraught to want anyone around, even someone sympathetic. "No thanks. I'll be okay. But you could do something else for me. For Will actually, could you call your Dad and tell him? Vince too. I just can't – I don't –"

"I understand. Will do. And I'll call you as soon as I know anything."

When Mark hung up, Robyn hugged the phone to her chest. Mark's shocked response, along with his concern for Will and for her, pushed her moment of doubt into the background. This was the Ryder family she knew – warm, forthright, honest – just one of the many reasons she'd decided to marry Will. No matter what her father said, she trusted Will, and she trusted his family.

Nearby someone harrumphed. Robyn started. Special Agent Rolland stood next to the sheriff's deputy, his professional demeanor of gloom and doom fully in place. When he saw he had her attention, he gestured to the front drive. "What's the code to open the garage door?"

Reluctantly she furnished him with the numbers. It was the date of the day she and Will had met.

"It's your husband's workshop, isn't it? And that's where he keeps his business records?"

"Yes." She considered keeping the information from him, but what was the point? They were searching the whole house. "They're in the loft in the garage."

She turned to leave for the bedroom, but he stopped her. "Mrs. Ryder? I'd like to ask you a few more questions."

"I don't have to talk to you, do I?"

"No, you don't." Agent Rolland was as unperturbed as usual by her response. "But what you tell me might help your husband."

But what if it incriminates him? The thought zoomed in on Robyn like an incoming missile, shattering her shaky defenses. "Y-Yes," she stuttered. "But – but I need to make some coffee first."

Rolland nodded. "I'll be back in five minutes. Deputy Simard here will keep you company."

You mean keep an eye on me! The thought irked Robyn, but she busied herself measuring the coffee, pouring in the water, getting the cream and mug. Should she talk to Rolland or not? Since Will was innocent, surely nothing she said would hurt him?

Unless he was guilty . . .

Distress shot through her. How could she think something like that? Unbidden, her father's accusations marched across her mind. She shut her eyes for an instant, only to spill steaming coffee on her hand. She dropped the mug. It shattered on the Saltillo tile floor, spewing glass and java everywhere.

When Rolland returned, Deputy Simard and she had just finished picking up the last of the coral colored ceramic pieces from the floor and mopping up the coffee.

She set the broom aside, poured herself another cup, and led the way to the dining room picnic table. She ignored her inclination to offer Rolland a cup. This man had just arrested Will!

They had barely settled at the table, when he started. "How long have you known Will Ryder?"

"Two-and-a-half years."

"Are you aware of any criminal activity on his part?"

"No."

Rolland pulled out a pad and flipped some pages. He appeared to be looking for something and after he found it, he nodded in satisfaction then looked up at her, his eyes glittering. "You do know that your husband grew up in the area known as "The Meadows"? One of his friends is in prison for armed robbery. Another two are in and out on drug charges."

Robyn's face flamed. "I know where he grew up." But she hadn't known about his friends from high school. Mostly he hung out with his brothers, and a couple of guys he'd met at Florida State.

"What about Ryder Brother's Construction? Do you know your husband's company is in financial straits?"

Robyn crossed her arms and glared at Rolland. "No, I don't know that. I do know that he's not doing as well as he'd like."

"That's an interesting way to describe it. Is it bad enough that he'd try to rip off your father?"

"Will would never do that." A muscle pulsed in her jaw, and she struggled to stay calm. "I've got my own business too," she said. "I know what it means to have cash flow problems. Losing two contracts isn't good, but it isn't the end of the world, either."

"Hmm." Elbows on the yellow and aqua tablecloth covering the picnic/dining table, Rolland rested his chin on his steepled fingers. "So you know about the contracts?"

"Yes." For a moment her father's angry accusations rang in her head, but she blocked them out. "I found out yesterday, at the same time Will did. Vince told us. He knew six days ago, the day before the wedding. He didn't tell us because he didn't want to spoil the wedding."

"And you believe that?" Rolland's heavy-lidded eyes narrowed.

"Of course. Why wouldn't I?"

In reply, the agent merely watched her. The silence lengthened, and Robyn suspected it was a calculated ploy to rattle her. She focused on her breathing and took a long, slow sip of coffee. She was shaky, yes, but after being kidnapped, blindfolded and tied up for three days, it would take more than a calculated silence to throw her off.

"Has your husband asked you for money?"

"No. We share expenses for the house, if that's what you mean, but we run our businesses separately."

"Would you give him money if he asked?"

Robyn nodded. "If I had it. Right now I'm putting most of my profits back into Island Fit."

"What about your father? Has your husband asked him for money?"

"Not that I know of." *But if he had, Raul would likely have turned him down.* The thought did not give her comfort.

"You co-own the house?"

"Yes. Will and I, and we've got a mortgage with the bank."

"Does Mr. Ryder drink?"

Robyn blinked. *What did that have to do with anything?* "Yes," she said slowly. "He enjoys beer, mostly on the weekends. Occasionally he'll have a scotch or vodka."

"And he uses the computer and printer in his office in the garage?"

"Yes."

"What for?"

"Writing up estimates, invoices, e-mail, that kind of thing. He also does some drafting."

"So you'd say he knows his way around a computer?"

Robyn paused. "Sure."

"Does anyone use the computer besides Mr. Ryder?"

"I've used it a couple of times since we moved into the house. So has Vince. But it's mostly Will."

"That's interesting." Rolland sat back in his chair, and his hound-dog face blossomed with a smug smile Robyn suspected didn't bode well for her or Will.

"And you didn't stay in the house the night before the wedding?"

"No. After the rehearsal party, I went to Izzie Sudak's house – my maid of honor. Will stayed here."

"So if I told you we found crumpled printed pages in the recycle bin the cleaning ladies took out of the house Saturday afternoon, it's most likely they were discarded by Mr. Ryder?"

"Most likely." Robyn frowned. "What are you getting at? What papers did you find in the garbage?"

The hint of sympathy in his eyes should have prepared her for his next words, but it didn't.

"Seems your husband had a little trouble finding the right words for the ransom notes. We found at least three versions of each note when we went through the trash."

CHAPTER SEVEN

People filled every available space on the benches in the courtroom at the Federal Courthouse on Simonton. As Will was escorted to the prisoner's box, hands and ankles shackled, he scanned the room for familiar faces. Vince, Mark and his father sat together in one of the front rows. His father's two older, unmarried sisters Marcy and Peggy sat in the row behind, their white hair and flowery pantsuits out-of-place in the dignified setting.

For one agonizing moment, Will thought Robyn hadn't come. Relief washed over him when he found her, seated beside her father. Her face pale and pinched, she looked as if she hadn't slept since his arrest. In fact, she looked as haggard as he felt. It had to be so hard for her to be here.

He sought out her gaze, and when their eyes met, he smiled his gratitude. She looked away.

Will flinched. *What?* She couldn't . . .

Then he understood. Raul. Beside her sat Raul, his arm draped protectively around her shoulders, his black-ice gaze drilling into him.

Had Raul gotten to Robyn? Was that it? At the very least, Raul thought he had stolen some of the ransom money. It wouldn't be much of a leap to believe he had planned the whole kidnapping and ransom. The fact that the police believed it too didn't help. Especially when Raul had never wanted his daughter to marry him in the first place.

But Will didn't care what Raul thought. All he cared about was what Robyn thought. If their marriage was to last – if it was to survive this crisis -- he needed to know that she believed him. That she knew he would never do anything like this to her or to her father.

His stomach churning, he looked around the courtroom. Sergei Kakovka, Raul's sidekick, was there too, his smarmy and far-too-appreciative gaze on Robyn and her father. At Robyn's other side sat Izzie, in a hot pink lululemon yoga outfit

Thank God. At least Robyn had one person with her who hadn't already written him off as an irredeemable criminal.

Everyone rose as the judge, a gray-haired woman wearing heavy black glasses, entered the room. With a speed and efficiency honed by long practice, she disposed of arraignment after arraignment. Though Mark had insisted Will would be released on bail, tension started to grow inside Will as first one, then a second of the four people brought up before him were refused bail and remanded in custody. Both men had previous criminal records and were accused of violent crimes, armed robbery and assault. But wasn't kidnapping considered violent? And this one had certainly involved a lot more money than the few hundred dollars the accused robber arraigned before him had taken at gunpoint.

Will shuddered and sought out Robyn again. With her zombie-like gaze, those dark circles under her eyes, she looked ill, far worse than when he had rescued her from the ocean off Wisteria Island. It hurt to see her like this, especially after all she'd gone through already. His mouth tightened into a grim line. He *had* to get out of jail. He *had* to see Robyn, to show her how much he loved her, to convince her of his innocence.

Finally his turn came. The charges were filed and the prosecutor, a world-weary man in his mid-fifties, requested bail of one million dollars. Mark quickly agreed to the pre-arranged sum; the maiden aunts had pooled their resources and offered to put up the money as soon as they'd learned of the charges against Will, and he had gratefully accepted. But the amount still shocked him.

The judge cleared her throat. "Bail is set at one million dollars. The accused will report twice a week to the police. He will live with his father John Ryder, and continue to go to work daily with his brother Vince Ryder."

The judge looked at Will over the top of her reading glasses. "The accused will have no contact of any kind with the alleged victim Robyn Ryder. That, Mr. Ryder, means no phone calls, no faxes, no text messages, no conversations of any kind. Do you understand the conditions?"

What? Will froze. Mark hadn't said anything about not seeing Robyn. At his brother's slight nod, he forced out a response. "Yes, Ma'am."

"Good." The judge turned to Mark. "Mr. Ryder? Make sure your client understands he's not to be within one hundred yards of Mrs. Ryder's place of work or of her residence. If he breaks that undertaking – or any other part of this order – he'll be back in jail, immediately.

"Court is adjourned." The judge rose followed by everyone else in the courtroom. When she exited, people began talking and filing out of the benches. Only Will stood frozen in place.

He couldn't see Robyn – at all?

≈ ≈ ≈

Robyn gasped and looked at Will. He had turned chalk white at the court order. Before the hearing, her biggest worry had been that he might be kept in jail. But now? To not see him? To not be able to communicate with him in any way? Despite her confusion, despite the ugly doubts sown by his arrest, this wasn't what she wanted.

She hardly noticed as Raul urged her into the aisle and out into the hallway. "What is wrong with American justice?" he muttered as they moved along. "They should keep him in jail. No, jail is too good for him. They should hang him up by the –"

In the hallway, she saw Mark in a knot of Ryders: Will's father, brother Vince and his two aunts, all of them looking worried and tense. She wrenched away from Raul and made her way through the crowds to Mark.

"Why did the judge order Will to stay away from me?" she demanded.

Mark grimaced. For a moment he looked so much like Will that it hurt to look at him. Mark placed a gentle hand on her shoulder. "It's standard, I'm afraid. Kidnapping is a serious crime, and you're the victim. The courts don't like to have the alleged perpetrator in contact with the victim."

"But what about Will's workshop? All his things?" Robyn's voice cracked.

Will's father nodded sadly. "It's all right, Robyn. Vince will go get his tools and some clothes. The police have Will's truck, anyway."

Mark squeezed her arm. His blue eyes, brimming with sympathy and so like Will's, held her attention. "Don't worry. We all know Will didn't do it. Police aren't saying, but it looks like all the evidence is circumstantial."

Robyn lapped up the reassurances of which she'd been in desperate need ever since Will's arrest and Special Agent Rolland's news about the notes in the recycle bin. She trusted Will, but events had shaken her confidence. It didn't help that an enraged Raul had already tried, convicted and sentenced him, or that he'd spent the whole of last night railing about the depravity of his son-in-law.

Her father chose that moment to push his way into the circle of Ryders. "What about my money?" he demanded. "How did that money get into your son's closet?" He glared at John Ryder.

Mark's expression flattened. "I don't know, Mr. Leopoldo. That's one of the many things we need to investigate."

"Well, I know." Raul straightened to his full height. His black eyes flashed and he jabbed a finger in John Ryder's chest. "*Ladrón,* a thief, that's what your son is. A thief and a bastard. He's not good enough for –"

"Raul!" Robyn snapped. "Stop it. Now."

"Why?" Raul threw up his hands. "Everything I say is true. He has kidnapped you. He has stolen my money. Worst of all, he's hurt you, *mi amor,* and for that he can never pay enough."

Mark ignored Raul and spoke to Robyn. "I'll call you later today, all right?"

She nodded and turned to look for Izzie. Her head was pounding. She felt as if she was being torn apart. She had to get out of here. Izzie stood waiting against the wall.

Robyn almost cried out in relief. "Have you got your car? How about a ride to the club?"

"Sure. I'll –"

Raul interrupted. "You should go home. You haven't slept. You haven't eaten. You look terrible."

It took all Robyn's willpower not to scream at her father. She gritted her teeth and reminded herself that he meant well, that rightly or wrongly, he still thought of her as the little girl he'd left behind so many years before. For a moment she wished her mother were still alive. She would know what to do.

But she wasn't. With a colossal effort, Robyn responded to her father in a calm voice. "You're probably right. But I can't go there yet. Not when . . . not if . . .

She swallowed hard, cutting off the sob that tried to burst loose from her throat. "I need to go to work. That's all."

"All right *mi amor*." The anger faded from Raul's face. His tone gentled. "When will you go home?"

On the heels of his rage, the tenderness was almost more than Robyn could take. "Around eight. Izzie will give me a lift."

"No." Raul shook his head. "Sergei and I drove you here. We will take you home. I'll bring my things from the hotel. I will not leave you alone in that house."

"I'll be fine, Raul," Robyn protested. For the first time since they entered the courtroom, she noticed the big Russian hanging back behind her father several steps. "I'm just going to go straight to bed when I get there. It's not necessary for you to leave your hotel."

Raul straightened. "You are my daughter, *mi querida hija*. Of course it is necessary."

His face darkened again. "Someone has to protect you from that thieving *hijo de puta*."

≈≈≈

When Robyn stepped out of the courthouse, microphones poked at her face, lights flashed, and questions flew at her from every side from reporters perched on the steps.

"Mrs. Ryder, did your husband kidnap you?"

"Robyn! How are you handling the shock of your husband's arrest so soon after your abduction?"

"Is it true the ransom money was found in the home you share with the accused?"

Robyn's first reaction was to shield her face from the cameras and recording equipment and run. Izzie tried to push her through the crowd of microphone and notepad wielding reporters, but at the last moment Robyn decided against it. She lowered her arms and planted her feet.

"Look," she said slowly and clearly, "I don't know any more than you do. All I can say right now – all I'm willing to say right now – is that I love my husband and have no reason to believe he had anything to do with my abduction. And now, if you don't mind, I'm very tired and need to go home."

She hoped her statement would put an end to it, but it didn't. The moment she stopped speaking, the reporters fired off more questions. Questions she didn't dare answer for fear they would reveal the cracks in her faith in Will.

She looked at Izzie. Her friend nodded. Together they pushed their way through the reporters and cameramen and sprinted for Izzie's bright red Jeep Wrangler. Only one cameraman pursued them, while the rest turned their attention to Raul and Sergei, who had followed them out.

As Robyn slammed the door and Izzie revved the engine, she saw her father gesticulating wildly to the reporters. She winced. Since her abduction he had become so much more vociferous in stating his views. He was probably painting Will as a low life who had broken his daughter's heart for cold, hard cash. She should go back and dispute what he was saying, but she didn't know if she could carry it off. Not in the face of the doubts that kept pushing up their ugly little heads when she least expected it.

"Drive," she ordered Izzie, and drive she did, squealing through the high black gates of the parking lot. Once out of the lot however, Izzie got caught behind the Conch train slithering around the narrow Old Town streets bulging with cruise ship tourists and slowing down to a crawl at every historical sight. Then of course there was the maddening issue of dodging both tourists and locals riding their bikes haphazardly down the middle of the streets and walking against the lights. They finally pulled into the almost empty lot at Island Fit on Eaton save for scooters, bikes and adult tricycles that were becoming more the vehicle of choice with her older clients.

She sighed and headed for the entrance. Under a royal blue canopy, the double glass doors gleamed, their gold script lettering proclaiming "ISLAND FIT – Your key to good looks and good health". Normally, seeing the doors that Will had installed filled her with love and pride, but today it all seemed a little tawdry. She noticed that some of the gilt lettering in "ISLAND" had chipped away.

Inside they were met by a rush of cool air, and a friendly hello from Candice, the college student manning the check-in desk in the lobby. The building was bright and airy, and decorated in soothing but upbeat shades. The renovations that Robyn, Izzie and Will had worked out had changed a drab, utilitarian gym into a place of beauty that complemented the programs they offered and made selling memberships relatively easy. At the moment the place was almost empty. In another hour, the club would be bustling with staff from nearby restaurants and bars as the shifts changed and some came off the day shift and some got ready for the craziness of a downtown Key West night shift.

Normally Robyn stopped to chat with Candice or whoever was on duty at the desk. Not today. She headed past the café tables in the lobby to the office she and Izzie shared, the largest in a row of offices on the left side of the building. Once inside, she pulled the shade on the window overlooking the treadmills, cross-trainers and rowing machines lined up below a bank of flat screen TVs. She plopped into her chair, and buried her head in her hands.

"Hey, hon, can I make you some chamomile tea?" Izzie asked.

"Please." Robyn didn't raise her head from her hands, but the sounds of Izzie bustling around making hot soothing tea were comforting. Thank God for Izzie. Robyn still didn't understand why her friend had refused to go in with her on buying the club where they both worked, but at least she had stayed as manager. What would she ever do without her, especially now?

Finally the tea was steeped. Gratefully Robyn cupped her hands around the mug, soaking up the warmth and the calming aroma. She took several slow sips before putting down her mug.

Izzie leaned against her desk, the pink yoga outfit flattering her dusky skin and cocoa eyes. She may have been a touch too plump to be a good example as a personal trainer, but her dimpled cheeks and welcoming smile made her a hit with members. Besides, she was a whiz with numbers, and drove a hard but fair bargain with everyone who worked at the club.

But to Robyn, none of that really mattered. They'd been fast friends since college, when the girl with the ugly scar on her cheek and the chubby girl with frizzy hair had the good fortune to find themselves roommates. Izzie had been there when Robyn's mother died, she had helped Robyn realize her dream of owning a fitness club and she'd cheered on her romance with Will and the search for her father.

"Thanks so much for coming to the hearing today," Robyn said quietly. "I – you don't know how much it means to me."

Izzie shrugged and moved to the window. She fiddled with the blind then pulled it up until she could observe the rows of aerobic equipment and the weight machines to her left.

"I can't believe this is happening," Robyn continued. "Not to Will, not to us. I mean, you go to bed one day, everything's great. You wake up and your life's turned into a nightmare."

She raked her fingers through her hair and looked at Izzie's back. On the other side of the glass, a lithe blonde in a royal blue Island Fit tank top and matching shorts walked by.

"Who's that?" Robyn asked.

"It's the woman I hired to replace Laura." Izzie turned around, her expression sober. "She started yesterday."

"Oh." Robyn rubbed her eyes. How could she have forgotten about Laura? "Why didn't you tell me what happened? I still can't believe Laura stole a member's wallet."

Izzie frowned and squeezed her hands together. "I'm sorry. I should have told you. I know how much you like Laura. But I hated to give you bad news right before the wedding."

Robyn shook her head. Everything associated with the wedding was turning into bad news. She gulped down more tea.

"Why didn't you call the police?"

"I thought it was better to handle the theft quietly. You know, bad publicity for the club." She made a face. "I guess it's my fault. Because this isn't the first time."

Robyn sat up straighter. "What do you mean, not the first time?"

The hand twisting continued. "One night after Easter, a wallet fell out of Laura's jacket pocket as she was leaving. I picked it up and was about to hand it to her when I realized it was Mrs. Richter's – you know, Joan Richter, the retired teacher who comes here most afternoons? I recognized it because she'd bought some protein bars that day and had set the wallet on the counter. It had this little apple sticker on it. Laura insisted it was a mystery to her how it ended up in her pocket, but come on, I'm not an idiot. I warned her and then, well, look what happened last week."

Yeah, all hell broke loose! Robyn grimaced. If this was Izzie's idea of how to cheer her up, she had picked the wrong topic. Finding out someone she'd thought was a great employee and a good friend was actually a thief was discouraging. And then the charges against Will . . .

She groaned. "Forget about Laura. How are we going to help Will? Especially when I can't even talk to him."

Izzie pulled the chair from her desk over to where Robyn sat and plopped down into it. She sighed. "I hate to say this, but maybe it's best if you just sit tight and see what the FBI comes up with."

"But this is Will. *Will*, Izzie. I love him. I just . . ."

"I know, sweetheart." Izzie's dark eyes brimmed with sympathy. "The charges hit me really hard too, especially after your kidnapping. But if there's a problem, maybe it's better to find out now, before it's too late."

"What do you mean, "IF there's a problem"?" Robyn's voice rose. "This is Will Ryder we're talking about. Mr. Good Nature, donates time and materials to Habitat for Humanity, good with children and animals, wouldn't hurt a fly. Will, for God's sake."

The hand twisting started up again. "But his business partner is Vince."

"Yeah? And?" Izzie had dated Will's older brother for a couple of months shortly after she and Will had started seeing each other, but it had fizzled out.

"Well, you know Vince used to be with the Key West Police?"

"That's right." Robyn frowned. "But he'd already left by the time I started dating Will."

"You know why he left?"

"Not exactly. It was a personal problem, something to do with gambling. That, and Vince is a terrific carpenter and all around very capable handyman. Will wanted him for the business."

"There's more to it than that. Sure Vince had a problem – a gambling addiction. Even he admits that. But there was talk he took bribes from some unsavory people. That's what did him in."

Robyn winced. "And you're telling me this now, why?"

Izzie's expression grew earnest. "Because you should know that Will, however much he cares about you, hasn't been entirely up front about his family. Maybe even about his own past. We both know where he grew up and the guys he hung out with when he was younger. Who knows what skeletons he's got in his closet."

"I can't believe you're saying this. I thought you liked Will."

"I do." Izzie took Robyn's hand. "But you're my best friend and I don't want to see you hurt."

Her eyes held Robyn's. "That's why, before you go off spouting about his innocence, you need to take a step back and take a really good look at everything you know about Will."

CHAPTER EIGHT

"What do I have to do to see Robyn?"

Will looked at his brother expectantly. No matter what the court order said, there had to be a way.

"You can't see her, end of story."

"Ah, c'mon, Mark. You can't mean that."

"Oh, but I do."

Mark took off his suit jacket and hung it over the back of the wooden kitchen chair. Though the hearing had ended in the mid afternoon, it had been after six by the time Will had been processed and allowed to leave the jail. After a quick stop to pick up a sandwich at the nearby grocery store, he and Mark and John Ryder had returned to his father's conch house in The Meadows.

His father had gone out back to water the beefsteak tomatoes, lettuce and spinach he'd been growing as long as Will could remember.

He and Mark sat in the kitchen at the table. The room was small and clean, like everything else in the small house, but it also smelled of cigarette smoke from the pack a day of Marlboro Lights John Ryder smoked. Unlike his three sons, each of whom had flirted with smoking as teenagers but had eventually kicked the habit, he insisted he would die smoking. And he probably would. Will suspected he'd be spending a lot of time outside on the front porch to get away from the smoke.

"No, I mean it, Mark. I've got to see Robyn. I'm worried about her. She looked so awful in the courtroom and she wouldn't even look at me. I need to know what she's thinking."

"She knows you're innocent," Mark responded. "She said as much after the hearing. And she's as upset as you are that she can't see you."

Will searched his brother's face. "I hope so," he said slowly. "But you didn't see her in the courtroom. When I caught her eye, she turned away. She turned away, Mark. And Raul was right by her side, glaring at me as if I was a serial killer. He's probably been at her every minute since my arrest trying to convince her that I'm the devil. Or worse."

"Hey, don't take it so hard. Robyn's known you a long time – longer than she's known her father. She's not going to desert you. If it makes you feel any better, I'll talk to her again. You won't do yourself – or her – any favors by getting hauled back into custody."

Will knew Mark was right, but it didn't make him feel any better. He hated not being able to act, not being able to see Robyn. But if he couldn't see her, there had to be at least something he could do to support his case.

He leaned forward. "All right. So I won't see Robyn. What's next? What do we do to start proving my innocence?"

"*We* don't do anything. It's better if I hand your case off to another criminal lawyer."

"What?"

Mark held up his hand. "I know what you're thinking, but it has nothing to do with my belief in you. It's just better if the person representing you isn't related. I'm too close, Will. I'm your baby brother, for Christsakes. What if

I miss something? I don't want you to end up in prison because I screwed up. I've already spoken to Dave Federenko. You know, the guy who handled that double murder case up the Keys last year? He's agreed to take you on."

Will frowned. "You're forgetting one thing. Money. I'm not exactly rolling in cash, and these charges aren't going to help bring in new business."

Mark grinned. "The aunts have it all taken care of."

"You mean Marcy and . . ." Will shook his head. "No way. They've already put up the money for my bail. I can't ask them to pay my legal bills too."

"They want to do it, Will. Hey, the last thing they want to see is their favorite nephew in prison. Besides, you're in their wills. Just consider it an advance on your inheritance."

Will frowned. "I don't like it. I —"

"Don't knock it. Take it as a sign. You know the aunts like to bet on the horses. They've won thousands over the years, and even more in the last couple of years at Pompano Beach. And you know how they do it? They always pick winners."

Mark stood up and swung his jacket over his shoulder. "Guess that makes you a winner, pal."

Will shoved his chair away from the table and stood up. "Yeah, if I was a horse."

≈≈≈

Mopping sweat from the back of her neck, Robyn stuck her head into the office. Izzie sat at her desk, confirming the staff schedule for the next week. "Can I borrow your car, Izzie? I want to take a quick run over to Finnegan's."

Izzie pulled open a desk drawer, retrieved her keys and tossed them to Robyn. "Say hi to George for me."

"I will." George McMaster had been her late mother's business partner and boyfriend. They had never married, never even lived together, but he'd played father to Robyn in all the ways that counted. If she hadn't tracked down Raul a few months ago, George would have been the one to walk her down the aisle. Instead, he had graciously stepped aside to allow Raul the father-of-the-bride honors he so clearly craved. No one had been more devastated by her abduction than George, who had berated himself to anyone who would listen for leaving the reception just minutes before it happened.

But now she needed George's counsel. Quiet and dependable, he had always been generous with his help. Robyn had hoped that leading the yoga class would take her mind off Will, but it hadn't worked. More than once she'd lost her way, awkwardly sitting at the front of the class trying to figure out where she was in the routine while the participants shared sympathetic glances and nervous smiles. Everyone knew she had been kidnapped. Everyone knew Will had been arrested, and why.

Ten minutes later, showered and dressed in tan shorts and an Island Fit t-shirt she had stashed in her gym bag, Robyn drove Izzie's jeep up Eaton towards Finnegan's Wake Irish pub. A local landmark, Finnegan's was at the edge of the entertainment district and owned by George. Tonight, Friday, it would be busy, but George would make time for her. He always had, ever since she'd been a child, doing her homework in the backroom while she waited for her mother to finish up.

She was lucky to find a parking spot on Grinnell Street and hurried into the pub. The dark interior, rich with mahogany wainscoting, wonderful bar with gleaming brass foot rails, had all the rich comfort and welcoming ambiance of an upscale Irish pub. Despite the bustle and noise, Robyn felt better the moment she stepped inside.

Bypassing the hostess, she made her way straight to the bar. George, shirtsleeves rolled up to his elbows, glided from one end of the bar to the other, filling orders, mixing cocktails, joking with the locals and tourists in the light Irish accent he had kept up, despite spending all but the first two of his sixty years in Florida. The moment he saw her, he set down a glass and leaned across the bar. "Wol'll ye be havin' me girl?"

"I need to talk to you. Can we . . ." Robyn nodded to the back room.

"Done." George instructed the other bartender to fill in for him. He took off his apron, tossed it under the bar, and ducked through the doorway towards the backroom. Robyn paralleled his movements to meet up with him.

The moment the door to his private office shut behind them, the stocky man with the brush cut and lined face dropped his Belfast imitation and held out his arms. Without hesitation, Robyn went to him. She buried her face in his boney shoulder, inhaling the yeasty odor of beer and wine and smoke she had associated with him as long as she remembered. His arms closed around her and he rocked her back and forth. "Oh, my little girl, my sweet little girl," he murmured.

After a moment, Robyn composed herself and prepared to face him. She pulled back. "You know about Will, then?"

The furrows in his unkempt brow grew deeper and for the first time ever, Robyn thought he looked far older than his sixty years. "I saw it on the telly, yes. They've been flashing the news on and off ever since the bail hearing this afternoon. I'm so sorry, Robyn. This is terrible."

Robyn slumped onto the scuffed and ripped leather sofa where she'd napped more than one afternoon away as a child. "The worst part is not being able to see or even talk to Will. And Raul is ready to kill him on sight. The police believe Will arranged the abduction for the money. Even Izzie is suspicious of him."

George sat down beside her. She braced for either an onslaught of advice or another attack on Will. But all George said was, "What do you think?"

She sighed. "I want to believe Will, so badly. I know that he loves me, and there's nothing in the last few months that would make me think otherwise. But . . ."

"But?" George raised his bushy white eyebrows.

"But I made a horrible mistake when I ran off and married Ralph right after high school. I thought that I'd grown up, that I'd learned so much, that I was a good judge of character now. I was so careful with Will. I waited so long to even consider marriage again. I don't know how I could be wrong about him. But maybe . . . maybe I have been. Maybe I am."

George got an odd look in his dark gray eyes. Then, "You don't really believe that, do you?"

"No," she admitted. "What's happening now just seems so unreal, like a bad, bad dream . . . but it isn't."

"I don't know Will as well as you do, but I have to agree. I lived around the corner from his family for years. John Ryder was always a bit of a drifter, moving from job to job, drinking hard, playing hard. But when his wife died, and he was left with those three youngsters, he shouldered his responsibilities and provided a better home than anyone expected. To be sure, the boys all got into their share of scraps, but nothing really serious. And look at them now – the youngest a lawyer, and Will and Vince in business together. The Will Ryder I know would never do anything like this, least of all for money."

Robyn pressed her hands together until they hurt. "Mark says the only evidence against him is circumstantial. But there are no links to anyone else. The police have checked out the employee who wrote the note that brought me out of the tent Saturday night, and they're convinced it's just a coincidence."

She didn't mention Laura's thefts from club members, or that this was one more case where she'd misjudged someone she thought was a friend. It hurt to even think about it.

"And then of course, there's Ralph."

"Hmm." George paused. "You haven't given him more money, have you?"

"No. Not since the six thousand dollars I loaned him four months ago so he wouldn't lose the store. But he phones me up every couple of weeks, usually when he's had too much to drink. He starts off wheedling, then when I won't give him anything, he cusses and calls me names."

"The police know about him too?"

"Yes."

For a long moment George said nothing. Then he patted her hand. "Perhaps the best thing you can do now is being patient. So much has happened in the last week. Be patient. Be strong. For you, and for Will. I know you can do it." He straightened, and Robyn knew she was in for one of the gentle lectures he had given her for years.

"Don't let the mistakes you made as a child paralyze you now. And you were a child when you ran off with Ralph. Since then you've grown into a smart, strong, beautiful woman more than capable of making her own decisions. But every decision, no matter how well thought out, involves some risk. That's the nature of life. If you remain paralyzed by fear, you'll never take a chance, never commit to anyone, never have a child. Don't let fear rule your life."

George's voice had risen with each word until he broke off and sat back self-consciously, his face red. Robyn suspected he wasn't talking about just her anymore, but she didn't press him.

"Are you hungry?" George picked up the phone.

She started to protest but remembered she hadn't eaten all day. And when she cleaned off her favorite menu item, a heaping plate of Shepherd's Pie under his watchful eye, she felt stronger and more composed than she'd been all day.

"You're too good to me," she said as she stood to kiss him goodbye.

"Irish Bread Pudding?" His gray eyes twinkled as he suggested her special weakness.

"Thanks but I've got to run. Raul's picking me up at the club at eight."

Nothing had changed, but her visit with George had energized her. Will's prospects no longer seemed so bleak, and she was itching to do something about it. As she opened the door to Izzie's jeep, she glanced at her watch. Only seven-thirty. Time still to pay a quick visit to her ex-husband Ralph. Kleiner's Electric was down the street, only a few blocks from Island Fit. If she hurried, she could zip in, ask him a few leading questions, and be back at the club in plenty of time. Even if he wasn't involved, he might have heard something about it.

Except for handfuls of tourists wandering the streets deciding on which type of wonderful watering hole they would choose, the bustle had died down. As she got out of the jeep, she took a good look at the store her ex-husband had taken over after his parents retired and moved to Arizona. It had once been the best electrical supply store in town, but since Ralph's takeover and the arrival of the big box stores, it had fallen on hard times. Paint peeled off the ornate gold and brown sign. One of the wires suspending a golden light bulb above the plate glass window had snapped, and the bulb listed to one side, banging into the glass when the wind was just right. Robyn smiled to herself as this seemed kind of ironic.

The bell chirped overhead as Robyn entered the store. Inside the display of tools, equipment and specialty bulbs were dusty and disorganized. Everything reeked of neglect, the same neglect that Ralph showed for himself and everyone around him. A male clerk, a long-haired high school student, came hurrying from the back to the front desk, tucking in the tails of his gold and brown shirt as he approached. "Can I help you, ma'am?"

Robyn shook her head. "Is Ralph in?"

"He's in the back."

Robyn started for what had once been the stockroom, but now served triple duty as office, warehouse and bedroom since Ralph had sold his parents' house.

"You can't go back there. Mr. Kleiner is busy."

"It's all right. He'll see me." She pushed past him. She rapped on the door then pushed it open. Ceiling high rows of shelving ran from a narrow aisle to the back wall of the store, all of them crammed with dusty boxes of who knows what. "Ralph?"

Her voice cracked, and she frowned. After all this time, she couldn't still be afraid of him, could she? She touched the scar on her left cheekbone and straightened.

No response, but she knew he was here. She proceeded to the last row of shelves. Behind it was an old-fashioned oak desk and a totally out of place floral chintz yard sale sofa piled high with a mixture of dirty and clean clothing. And behind the desk, his swivel chair pushed back and his feet up, was Ralph.

Shock coursed through Robyn, the same shock she'd experienced every time she'd seen Ralph Kleiner in the last few years. At six-foot-two and the star running back of their high school's football team, the Fighting Conchs, he had always been big and strong. Now he was just big. Years of junk food, beer guzzling, and inactivity had turned muscle to fat. His thick, wavy hair had thinned to pathetic blonde wisps combed across his balding head, and the sharp contours of his once-handsome face had disappeared under a puffiness that reflected his dissolute lifestyle. He looked closer to forty than thirty. But in the midst of the folds of skin, his blue eyes were sharper and far more alert than she had expected, given the can of Miller in his hand and the dozen or more empties littering the floor.

Ralph's eyes flickered, but he took another gulp of beer before acknowledging her presence. "So what brings Little-Miss-Too-Good-To-Talk-To-Me here at this hour?" The ugly sneer on his face echoed in his voice. "Oh, I know. It must be that she's not so high-and-mighty any more. That her new husband has turned out to be not so perfect after all. That maybe I'm not looking quite so bad any more."

Each word cut, but Robyn forced herself to ignore Ralph's slurs. Nothing he said could make anything worse than it already was. She nodded. "You're right. Terrible things have happened, and I do need your help. You've lived in Key West your whole life. You know lots of people. Can you think of anyone who has it in for Will or me? Someone who'd kidnap me and try to set him up to take the blame?"

Ralph laughed, his whole body jiggling with the effort.

"What's so funny?" snapped Robyn.

He took another swig of beer then wiped his mouth with the back of his hand. "You? Asking *me* for help? As if."

Robyn went rigid with anger. She'd like to slap him, but what would that prove? Besides, she didn't like to get too close. In the ten years since she'd left him, she'd worked at developing toughness of body and mind, while his physical and mental powers had deteriorated. No more defenseless victim for her! But he was at least three hundred pounds, and size alone might give him the ability to hurt her yet.

"Why not?" she countered. "I helped you with that loan a few months ago."

"Yeah, and made me beg for every cent of it." With surprising swiftness for such a big man, he swung his feet to the floor and sat up straight. "You haven't exactly helped me since then, either."

"No." Robyn paused. "But I could, if you were able to help me in return."

He snorted, downed the rest of his beer and tossed the can onto the floor. He picked up another, popped the top, and drank some more. "You really think I'm stupid, don't you? After all you've done to me, you think you can buy my help?"

Before she could say anything about his twisted view of the past, he swung his feet back onto the desk and leaned back in his chair. "Well, I've got news for you. I don't *need* your two-bit help. You can't bribe me. I've got me a new silent partner."

"A silent partner? Who?" Despite herself, Robyn was curious.

Satisfaction gleamed in Ralph's little pig eyes. "Wouldn't be silent if I told you, now, would it he slurred? Besides, it's none of your business. I've got big plans for Kleiner's Electric, you'll see."

"Well, good for you. I guess that means you'll be paying me back soon."

"Maybe." Ralph was cagey enough not to commit himself. Robyn had assumed when she lent the money she'd never see it again. But she wasn't ready to give up on pumping him for information. He had been a violent, spoiled young man, but also sly, motivated, and charming when the situation called for it. Surely there was some goodness left in him?

"Please, Ralph. I'm begging you. If you've heard or seen anything – anything at all – that might prove Will's innocence, please tell me. No one needs to know the information comes from you."

Ralph shrugged. "No can do. Now if you don't mind, the evening's young, and I've got things to do." He nodded at the case of beer.

Robyn sighed. "One last question. Where were you last Saturday night – my wedding night?"

Ralph raised his beer in a silent toast. "You should have asked me to your wedding, sweet cheeks. Then you'd know where I was. But I'll give you a break. The police already asked me that, and they were so satisfied with my answer they went out and charged Will with your kidnapping. Great, huh?"

"Yeah, wonderful." Robyn stomped out, slamming the door behind her.

≈ ≈ ≈

After Robyn dropped the Jeep off at the gym, she prepared herself for the ride home with her father. The call on her ex had sapped her short-lived burst of energy and optimism, and now all she wanted to do was crawl into bed and pull the covers over her head. But in an effort to divert

Raul from another rant against Will, she forced herself to make small talk.

"Where's Sergei? I thought you said he was coming too."

"Not tonight. He needs to make several international and cross-country calls on my behalf. I should have left for Denver three days ago. Instead, I'm flying out tomorrow. Sergei will come and stay with you while I'm gone."

"That's really not necessary." Robyn ran hot and cold when it came to Sergei. Sure, he'd helped pull Raul away from Will. But his habit of standing far too close and his occasional overheated glances and leading smiles made her uncomfortable.

"There are houses on both sides of mine," she continued. "The neighbors are there at night, and the new security system has just been installed. I don't need a bodyguard."

"*Mi querida hija.*" Raul shook his dark head. He had regained the calm that had deserted him last night and this afternoon after the bail hearing. "Can you not humor an old man? We have been apart so long. So much of your life I have missed, so little I have been able to do for you. This is a small thing, easily done. And it would make me feel . . . useful."

His black eyes met hers and his lips turned up in a faint smile. "Important in your life."

His words were a gentle reminder of the pain of separation he had suffered during the twenty-seven years apart from his wife and daughter. It was a pain Robyn had known nothing about until after her mother's death, when she'd discovered the cache of letters from Raul to her mother. Letters in which he professed, over and over, his love for her mother and begged her to come back to him. It was because of those letters – and the pain and sorrow expressed there – that she had embarked on the search for the father she didn't remember, and about whom she knew little.

It was that pain, now, that made her soften towards him. "Oh, Raul. You really don't need to do this. But all right. For you, I'll accept Sergei's presence. Not for me. For you."

He smiled broadly, and light flashed off a gold tooth in the upper right side of his mouth, something she'd never noticed before. Her gaze lowered to the ring on his right pinkie finger, a wide gold band studded with three brilliant emeralds surrounded by tiny diamond chips.

He noticed her interest and moved his hand closer so she could see the ring better. "These emeralds are from one of my mines in Colombia – the best emeralds in the world." His hand returned to the wheel. "Would you like something similar?"

"Oh, no." Did he think she was angling for a ring? He'd paid for the wedding – and the ransom – that was more than enough. She stuffed her hands between her thighs. The only ring she wore was a plain gold wedding band, a match for the one on Will's ring finger. For months Will had tried to convince her to pick out a diamond engagement ring, but she had refused, believing the money was better spent on the house and their businesses.

As they snaked around the streets to the Southernmost Point they passed several rundown gingerbread houses. Noticing a gabled widow's walk, stark against the sky, brought home Will's predicament. How could he have lost those two contracts? Both Vince and Will had believed they were in the bag. And now, after Will's arrest, how many more jobs would they lose? She needed to talk to Vince, to –

"I want to speak to you about your future," Raul said, interrupting her tortured thoughts.

"No, Raul, I think –"

"*No*, Robyn," her father retorted sharply. "Listen to me. Coming late to your life, I have been reluctant to interfere, especially in your marriage. I admit, I had some doubts about this Will Ryder of yours, but still, I remained silent because I could see that you cared deeply about him."

"What doubts?" Robyn had known there was friction between the two men, but until the argument she'd overheard outside the church, it had stayed in the background.

"I do not mean I thought he was a bad man, *mi amor*. But his business is not sound, and is getting worse. You deserve a man who can take care of you, a real man.

"But now – well, a man who would arrange to have his own wife kidnapped for money? A man who would endanger your life by stealing the ransom money? This is not a good man, *querida*. Not for you, or for any woman."

Robyn had to fight down the lump forming in her throat. "I know how it looks, Raul. Really bad. But his lawyer says the evidence against him is only circumstantial –"

"And his lawyer is his brother," interrupted Raul, his tone hard. "As likely as not he's part of the conspiracy."

104

Robyn inhaled sharply. She couldn't listen to this all night. She wouldn't. She remembered George's advice. Be patient. Be strong. "Raul, please," she remonstrated.

"I must speak, *querida*. It's too important. I would not be doing my duty as your father if I remained silent. You must know, it is possible to remove yourself from this situation now, before you are destroyed by it."

"What do you mean, remove myself?"

Raul jerked the wheel to the left and the car crunched over the stones of the driveway of her home before coming to an abrupt halt.

He turned and looked at her, his expression grave. "I want you to get an annulment. Either that or a divorce. We can get started on it tonight. I've already spoken to a lawyer."

≈≈≈

Mark packed the last of his notes and files concerning Will and the charges against him into a bulging briefcase then snapped the lock shut.

With a sigh, he stood up and stretched, rolling his shoulders back, stiff from tension and too much sitting. He looked out the second-floor window, onto an all but deserted Whitehead Street. His was one of several law offices situated in a restored conch cottage a few blocks from the Monroe County Courthouse. At midnight on Friday, it was likely the only one occupied. Everyone else, including his secretary Janice, had left many hours ago.

But then everyone else didn't have an older brother who'd just been charged with kidnapping his own wife. Shuddering at the thought, he turned away from the window and reached for his suit jacket, hanging on the back of his chair.

Watching Will brought into the courtroom this afternoon had been gut wrenching. Far worse than telling him that he wouldn't be defending him.

Mark shrugged into his jacket. It was for the best, and he knew it, though every irrational part of him screamed he was letting down his own blood. But he knew another lawyer, with no personal ties to Will, would be better able to analyze and weigh the threats against Will and devise the best plan of defense. And Dave Federenko was an excellent lawyer, with years more experience. He was aggressive and one-track minded on behalf of his clients, especially when he believed they were innocent. What more could an accused man ask?

Mark picked up the heavy briefcase then set it down again. There was no point taking it home. He'd be back here again at ten in the morning, along with Will and Federenko, to hand over the materials and discuss the next steps in Will's defense. And of course, he'd do whatever he could on the side to prove Will's innocence.

He turned off the lights in his office, then the reception area, and locked up. He hurried down the stairs and out onto the dimly lit street. There weren't too many lights in this part of town and, at the moment, no cars or pedestrians.

Hearing the band at the Green Parrot in the distance, he started across the street to his parked Lexus. He popped the driver's side lock with the remote when an engine blasted to life somewhere on his right.

He turned his head to look but it was already too late. The black SUV hit him straight on.

CHAPTER NINE

The instant Vince Ryder's cell phone number showed up on caller I.D., Robyn dropped the quilt she was pulling up over the bed and grabbed the phone from the night table.

"Vince," she gasped, her heart pounding. "Has something happened to Will?"

"No." Before she could catch her breath in relief, he continued. "It's Mark. A car mowed him down last night just outside his office."

"Is he okay?"

"He's in surgery now. Both of his legs are broken and he's got a concussion."

"Have the police got the driver?"

"No. It was a hit-and-run."

Robyn's stomach dropped. *Why this? Why now?* "You're at the Lower Keys Medical Center? I'll be right over." The medical center was on Stock Island, a fifteen-minute drive if the stoplights were in your favor.

There was a long pause. "Maybe that's not a good idea, Robyn. Dad and Sam are here, and so is Will." He paused again. "I'll call you again as soon as Mark's out of surgery."

"No." Her throat thickened. "No, I'm coming over," she insisted. "The judge didn't say anything about me staying away from Will, not at times like this. Besides, I'm not going to the hospital for him. I'm going for Mark."

She expected Vince to argue, but he didn't. "All right," he said softly. "When do you think you'll get here?"

"Fifteen minutes."

She said goodbye, grabbed her purse and headed for the kitchen. Raul sat at the counter, the Saturday Key West Citizen_spread before him, a mug of the strong, Cuban coffee he favored in his hand. Though it was Saturday, he wore a navy suit and tie in preparation for his flight to Denver later that morning. A black carry-on and hard-sided briefcase sat by his feet.

She leaned in to plant a quick kiss on his smooth olive cheek. "I'm off to the hospital. Mark Ryder was in a hit-and-run last night and has two broken legs."

She turned to go. Raul reached for her arm. "Is that a good idea? Won't Will and the rest of his family be there?"

Robyn straightened. Out of respect for her father's concerns, she'd put up with an hour-long lecture last night about why she needed to divorce Will. But this was different. "I don't care," she said quietly. "Mark is Will's lawyer. Mark is also my friend. I don't desert a friend when he needs me."

Any more than I'd desert Will right now. The thought startled her, but also gave her strength. Raul must have seen the conviction on her face; he didn't argue.

"All right then. But wait until I call Sergei. I'm leaving for the airport in a few minutes. He can come out and take you to the hospital."

She shook her head and gestured with her keys. "I'm taking my own car. See you next week when you get back."

≈≈≈

Ignoring the speed limit and passing the Saturday-morning dawdlers, Robyn made it to the hospital in just under fifteen minutes. She parked the car and hurried to the Emergency entrance. As she headed to the information window, a man wearing jeans and a white t-shirt stepped in front of her.

She gritted her teeth and started to sidestep when recognition struck. "Sergei!" She pulled up short. "What are–"?

She stuck her hands on her hips and glared at him. "Raul sent you, didn't he? Well, you can just leave. I don't want you here."

The big Russian shrugged and a dark flush rose up his thick neck and into his face. "You're right, of course. But your father asked me to come, and his association is important to me. As is the welfare of his daughter."

Robyn exhaled loudly. "I understand, but this is just too much. Go away."

Sergei nodded solemnly. "I would, but I can't. Not until I see Will."

"What? Why?"

"Your father told me that Mark Ryder is your husband's lawyer. While Raul does not approve of your husband or his crimes, for your sake, he wishes to ensure that Will is properly defended. On Raul's behalf, he's asked me to make an offer to Will."

"What kind of offer?"

"Raul is willing to pay for a new lawyer for Will."

"What?" Irritation turned to surprise. "He will?" Her eyes narrowed. "And the strings?"

"Strings?" Sergei blinked. "What are these strings you speak of? Oh." Understanding dawned. "No. There are no strings, only an offer of help."

His wry smile invited her to acknowledge Raul's authoritarian personality. "Yes, your father likes to be in charge. Of everything." His smile widened and his eyes sparkled with warmth. "But Raul is also a good man who cares deeply about your welfare. Because he knows how much Will means to you, he is willing to make this offer. To give Will every chance to redeem himself. For you."

Robyn's mouth fell open. Her annoyance with her father evaporated. He would do this, for her? "Let's go then. I can hardly wait to tell Will."

"You can't."

She halted. "What do you mean, I can't?"

"The court order, remember? You're not supposed to be anywhere near him."

"But –"

Sergei stared at her soberly. "Your father is willing to help Will. But he insists that you continue to obey the letter of the bail conditions. No, I will make the offer to your husband. You will continue to stay away from him."

Robyn opened her mouth to object then shut it. Given her father's dislike of Will, his offer was truly amazing. As much as she wanted to talk to Will, proving his innocence at this point was more important. With Mark out of the picture, she didn't know where he'd get the money for a good lawyer. Raul's offer might be his best chance.

"All right," she said slowly. "I won't talk to him. But you have to let me know if he accepts."

≈≈≈

Will saw Robyn first. He was on his fiftieth circuit of the waiting room when she rushed around the corner, flip flops slapping on the floor, dark eyes intent in a pale face surrounded by wavy hair that looked as if it had been blown dry in a wind storm. She clutched a pink and aqua plastic purse under the arm of her brightly flowered blouse, and car keys jangled in the pocket of her white Capri pants.

Gladness swelled up inside him as his gaze devoured her. God, she looked good! This past week he'd worried over her, ached for her, but it wasn't until this instant that he realized just how much she meant to him, how much ...

The spurt of joy disintegrated and fell to earth the moment he realized she'd seen him. Because instead of the heart-felt welcome he yearned to see from her, there was only a deep and shocking wariness. Her headlong advance halted as soon as her eyes met his.

And then, behind her, loomed a larger form. Sergei Kakovka! What was he doing here?

The Russian put his hand on Robyn's elbow and Will flinched. A bitter taste filled his mouth. This just gets better and better.

Someone nudged him from the left. He looked over. Vince's smile was weary, but encouraging. Sam, Mark's girlfriend, her face blotchy and creased from crying, clung to his arm.

"Son." John Ryder put a hand on Will's right shoulder and squeezed. His family's support eased the devastation he felt inside, but only a little.

Robyn approached, her face carefully composed. She addressed Will, but didn't quite look at him. "The surgery – is it over yet?"

"No. The doctor –"

Vince cut Will off. "Not for a while. Mark's legs were pretty badly mangled. We don't know yet how many rods or plates they'll have to put in."

"Oh." Robyn bit her lip. Will knew how fond she was of Mark. They'd spent a lot of time together with him and Sam, at the beach, dancing, biking around the island to try out the local's specials. Things Mark might not be able to do again for a long, long time.

"When . . . when did this happen?" She spoke barely above a whisper, each word vibrating with pain.

"Around midnight," John Ryder piped up from Will's right. "The son-of-a-bitch ran him down right beside his car. Lucky he didn't kill him."

"Was he conscious when they brought him in?"

Vince shook his head. "Yeah, but in shock. He kept talking, but it didn't make any sense. Couldn't tell the police anything worthwhile. There were no witnesses either. If a taxi driver hadn't driven by, God knows how long he might have laid there in the dark."

"But why would . . ."

Will answered the question all of them had asked themselves. "We don't know why, or who, or exactly how yet. The police are being pretty tight-lipped about the whole thing. They've got the accident site marked off, and they've taken away Mark's clothes to see if they'll reveal anything."

For the first time, Robyn met his gaze head on. Her liquid brown eyes shimmered with sympathy. "I am so sorry."

His chest constricted; for a moment he couldn't breathe. He wanted to hold her so badly, to —

Without warning Robyn flung her arms around a surprised Sam. "Oh, Sam. He'll be okay. I'm sure he'll be okay. I've been praying for him all the way in."

She released Mark's girlfriend, then hugged Vince and his father in turn. Finally she faced Will. Her lower lip trembled, and her eyes were bright with tears. "Will, I —"

Will couldn't stop himself. He stepped forward and pulled her into his arms. He hugged her fiercely, breathing in the sweet smell of her hair and skin. "I'm so glad you're here. You don't know how much."

At first, she was stiff in his arms. But then, with a swiftness that renewed his hope, she melted against him. Her arms circled his waist and her warmth flowed into him, far more comforting and life affirming than any medical procedure the hospital had to offer. Her lips brushed his cheek. "Oh, Will. How can this be happening? It's just . . . too much."

He stroked her hair as she clung to him. "I don't know," he murmured, knowing she was referring to far more than Mark's surgery. "But I do know that somehow, some way, we'll get through it all."

And for the first time in days he actually believed it.

≈≈≈

Another hour passed before the surgeon, a slight man in his early forties who looked like he had been up all night doing surgery, came out with the news of the successful operation. Mark's legs had been set, rods clamped for support to the femur in each of his legs. While the breaks were bad, and would necessitate a stay in hospital of at least a week, there was no internal injury and the MRI showed his concussion was light. Mark was in recovery now, and would be moved to a semi-private room later in the day.

"When will he be able to walk again?" Will asked the question on all their minds.

"Not for about four months." The surgeon frowned. "And he'll need physiotherapy. After a year or so he might want to come back in and have the rods removed. It depends on whether they bother him or not."

"But he will be able to walk again? To do everything he could do before?" Sam asked, her voice wobbling.

"I don't see why not. He may want to avoid some of the more extreme sports like kite boarding but he should be all right."

Tears started to stream down Sam's face. Will put his arm around her and wiped the tears away. "Hey, why the tears now? This is good news, Sam. Good news."

He looked up and met Robyn's eyes. She smiled, relief palpable on her face. She stood up, and Sergei, who'd been her shadow ever since she arrived in the waiting room, stood up too. Will subdued a stab of irritation.

"I'm going to the club for a couple of hours now," she said. "I'll come back to the hospital on my way home."

Will squeezed Sam's arm and turned to Robyn. "I'll walk you out to your car."

Vince frowned. "You'd better not." He glanced from Sergei to Will. "Don't push your luck."

"It's all right, Vince," Robyn intervened. "Sergei needs to talk to Will anyway."

"Sergei?" Will and Vince exchanged glances. "Why?" The Russian's faint smile revealed nothing.

"It's on behalf of my father. He flew to Denver this morning and didn't have time to come see you."

"Your father?" Will frowned. "If he has something to say to me, why doesn't he say it himself?"

"For me, Will. Please, talk to Sergei. It's important."

Will glanced at Sergei. The guy had always been friendly enough, but something about the way he looked at Robyn had always bothered him. Was he just being territorial, or was Sergei more interested in Robyn than he should have been? Was that it?

Will shrugged. "All right." He glanced at Vince and his father. "I'll be back in a few minutes. You want coffee?"

Robyn headed for the elevator, Will on one side, Sergei on the other. They waited for the elevator in silence, and descended in silence. In the lobby, Robyn turned to Will. "You'll still be here in a couple of hours?"

He nodded. "I want to see Mark awake before I leave."

"Good." She smiled and swung her purse over her shoulder. "I'll see you then." She looked at Sergei. "Are you going back to the house after this?"

He nodded.

After a lingering look that reignited all Will's yearning, Robyn turned away and slipped out the door. Will watched until she disappeared around the corner. He stuck his hand in his pocket to check for change then glanced at Sergei. "I'm heading for the cafeteria. You coming?"

"Certainly."

Sergei fell into step beside him, his long legs easily matching Will's stride. Out of the corner of his eye, Will noticed the man's muscular arms swinging by his sides. It was the first time he'd seen him in anything but a suit. The mining executive either worked out or pushed something bigger than a pencil on his job.

As they moved along the counter to the coffee dispensers, Will addressed Sergei. "So what's this message from Raul?"

Sergei glanced about while Will freed two Styrofoam cups from the holder. He filled first one, then the other, with steaming coffee.

"Raul is worried about Robyn. Ever since your arrest, she's barely eaten or slept. And now that Mark is injured and won't be able to act as your lawyer, she's worried you won't be able to afford another one."

Will added sugar and creamer to both coffees, then snapped on plastic lids. It was reassuring to know that Robyn worried for him, but not necessary. "She doesn't need to –"

"That's just it," Sergei interrupted. "Raul doesn't want her making herself sick over you. So he's instructed me to make you an offer."

Will fished the $4.50 for the coffee out of his pocket and handed it to the teenage cashier. He picked up the cups and looked at Sergei. "Yeah, I can imagine. What is it? Get out of town or I'll sue you for the ransom money?"

Sergei straightened. "It's not necessary to belittle my associate," he said sternly. "Raul's offer is very generous. He is willing to pay all your legal costs."

Will paused. "That is generous." His eyes narrowed. "So what's in it for him? He hates my guts."

"True." Sergei nodded. "But he loves Robyn. And of course, there is one proviso."

"Yeah?"

"Guilty or innocent, Raul will pay all your legal expenses. But only if you agree to an immediate annulment or divorce from Robyn."

CHAPTER TEN

It wasn't until the plastic lids popped off both cups and coffee flooded over the sides and onto his hands that Will realized he was crushing the Styrofoam.

He set the cups down on an empty table, shook off the coffee and replaced the lids, all the time struggling to control his urge to kick Sergei's butt.

Teeth clenched, he turned to the man. "I hope you're not going to try to tell me Robyn knows all about this."

The Russian didn't blink. "Of course she does. We spoke about it on the way up to the waiting room."

"You're lying." Nothing about Robyn's behavior indicated she wanted a divorce.

Sergei shrugged. "Believe what you want. But it's the only offer you're going to get."

Will picked up the half empty coffee cups. "Since you're acting as a messenger boy, you can give my answer to Raul."

"Yes?"

"Tell him to take his money and shove it."

Sergei didn't budge. "Isn't that unwise, my friend? Now that your brother's hurt, how will you pay for a lawyer?"

"That's none of your business."

Steaming, Will walked away and didn't look back.

≈≈≈

A sick employee kept Robyn from making it back to the hospital later that day. Izzie was off, and there was no one else available to man the desk. When Robyn finally raised Vince on his cell, he told her they'd left the hospital after a brief visit with Mark, who was still groggy from the anesthetic and spaced out from his morphine drip. He, Will and their father would return to the hospital later that evening for another quick visit.

A few minutes later the phone at the club rang again. It was Sergei. They agreed to meet at Finnegan's Wake for a late dinner after she closed up.

Shortly after eight o'clock, she walked into the pub. To her disappointment, George wasn't behind the bar.

Sergei sat at a booth at the back of the main room, a cigarette dangling from his lips and two empty shot glasses and a bottle of beer on the table before him. He stubbed out his cigarette when he saw her and patted the seat next to him. She pretended not to notice and slid onto a chair opposite him. It didn't take much more vodka before the Russian became amorous. She didn't want to encourage him.

If her avoidance bothered him, he didn't let on. "What can I get you to drink?" He waved the waitress over, and a moment later an iced tea was on its way.

Robyn leaned into the table. "So what did he say?"

"Who?"

"Will, of course. Did he accept Raul's offer?"

"No, he didn't."

Robyn sagged. "Why not?"

Sergei shrugged his broad shoulders. "He didn't want to discuss it, but I'd say it was just more of the same."

"More of the same?" Her voice rose. "What's that supposed to mean?"

"You know." Sergei picked at the beer label. "He and your father don't get along, especially now. I can't say I blame Will. I'd never take money from a man who thought I was a thief and a kidnapper."

"But he's not!"

Sergei hunched closer. His eyes bored into hers. "You may know that, Robyn, but face it. It's not what your father – or the police – think." He paused. "Besides, there may be another reason Will won't take the money."

"And what's that?"

"That he's feeling guilty." He shook his blond head. "I'm sorry, Robyn but I can't sugar coat the truth even for you."

Robyn bit back the protests that rose to her lips. Under the table she clenched her fists. Why was believing in Will such hard work? More and more, it was like clinging to a life raft being shot at from all sides. How much longer could she hang on? But then, what did she expect Sergei to say? He worked with her father, after all.

She opened a menu and stared at it until her anguish abated. It wasn't until the waitress had taken their orders, hers chicken pot pie which was her second favorite comfort food, his corned beef and cabbage, that either of them spoke again.

Sergei drank the last of his beer then set the bottle to the side. He tilted his head and studied her, his gray eyes intent. Robyn braced herself for another argument about Will.

"Have you given any more thought to your father's offer? And mine?"

She frowned. Presumably he meant the investment offer, not the offer to help Will. Within days of their first meeting, Raul had praised Island Fit as an excellent business with the potential to expand across Florida, and then the rest of the country. Robyn had been really excited when Raul and Sergei had both offered to invest in the company, and Izzie had walked around with dollar signs in her eyes. But after consideration, Robyn had turned them down. She wanted to expand, but the timing was wrong. She wanted to wait until the house was finished and she and Will had been married at least a year. This was her second marriage. She didn't want to screw it up.

"Not really. I loved the idea. I still do. But . . . but I can't. Not now. Not with so much going on."

"That's just it." Sergei pounded the table with his fist. "It would be a good distraction. Take your mind off your troubles. Besides, there's no guarantee the money will still be available later. We're both looking for new mining ventures. If one comes up before you decide, that's where the money will go."

Robyn grimaced. "I'm sorry. I just don't see how I can find the energy to do it right now."

"You know that's not the answer I want," he said gently. His gray eyes softened. "Don't shut the door completely. Please tell me you'll at least *think* about it."

His sudden tenderness threatened to push her over the edge, but she hung on. "All right," she said finally. "I promise to consider it. But don't get your hopes up."

His expression lightened and his broad mouth lifted in a smile. Until she felt the unexpected pressure of his hand on hers, she didn't realize he had moved closer to her.

"It's not my hopes that matter." His gaze burned into hers. "I just hate to see you hurting like this. If I can do anything to make it better . . ."

He didn't finish the sentence, but she knew he was talking about more than money and investments, more than fulfilling her father's wishes. She'd already fended off one drunken marriage proposal a couple of months earlier.

She slid her hand out from under his. "Thank you. I appreciate everything you're doing for me. I really do."

She gathered her resolve and looked him right in the eye. "But right now all my focus is on Will and his defense. I love Will. That isn't going to change any time soon."

Sergei's gaze narrowed ever so slightly. "Even if he's guilty?"

Robyn's heart sank. She didn't have an answer for that one.

≈≈≈

It was barely six forty-five Sunday morning when Robyn slung a Nike sports bag over her shoulder and headed out. She had dressed quickly in a white sports bra, black sweat pants with a matching black jacket, and her usual jogging shoes. In the bag was a towel and change of clothes.

As she reached for the doorknob, a voice rough with sleep chimed out from the living room sofa, "Hey, what's your hurry?"

She started guiltily, then composed herself and turned around. "Good morning, Sergei. I'm sorry if I woke you. There's no need for you to get up just because I can't sleep."

A lump formed in her throat as she took in his smooth bare chest, the Calvin Klein boxers slung low on his hips, the uncombed hair and unshaven jaw. Though the Russian's build was heavier and his personality entirely different from Will's, his physical resemblance was enough to provoke an unexpected and painful burst of longing. She swallowed hard and pasted a tight smile on her face.

"It's all right." Sergei yawned and a whiff of alcohol and cigarettes reached Robyn. He scrubbed a hand through his hair. "Where you going?"

"Since I couldn't sleep, I thought I'd go for a run at the cemetery, and then go into work for a few hours. The club doesn't open until nine a.m. Sundays, but there's always paperwork."

Sergei shook his head. "Wait up. I'll go with you."

"No. I'm in a hurry."

"But your father –"

"I don't need a babysitter, Sergei. It's already light outside, and by the time I get to the cemetery, it'll be full daylight. Besides, I want to visit my mother's grave, and I'd like to do it alone."

"Oh." Sergei blinked the sleep away. "I understand."

"Good. Why don't you go back to sleep?"

Robyn didn't wait for an answer. She slammed the door behind her, ran to her Zuma scooter, and headed out as quickly as she could. Actually, Sergei didn't understand, and it was better that way.

Vince had called on her cell last night while she was driving home from Finnegan's. Sergei, thank God, had remained downtown for a couple more hours, doing what she didn't know or care. What she did know was that Will needed to see her, and Vince had called to arrange a meeting at seven this morning, at the Key West Cemetery, near the short metal fence which housed her mother's headstone. She'd agreed immediately. She had to know why Will had refused Raul's money. How was he going to pay his legal expenses now that Mark was out of the picture?

As she slowly made her way through the deserted Old Town streets, she kept checking her rearview mirror. It was unlikely Sergei would follow her, but after this last week, she wouldn't bet on it or anything else. All the same, she was relieved when his blue BMW didn't materialize behind her.

She parked her scooter on Margaret, outside the high metal gates and sexton office marking the main entrance to the Cemetery. Will's black truck with the Ryder Brother's Construction insignia was nowhere to be seen, but then she remembered the police had taken it. She jogged through the metal archway, past the office on the left and down Palm Avenue bowing reverently at the U.S.S Maine and Los Martires de Cuba monuments as she passed by. She always smiled as she passed her favorite epitaph: "I told you I was sick." The stillness, broken only by the occasional crowing rooster and the thump of her running shoes usually soothed her, but not this morning. She was too worried about why Will wanted to see her. Normally she loved this cemetery, especially in the early morning before the oppressive humidity took over the lighter air. With its overabundance of prehistoric looking iguanas it had always seemed like the perfect waiting room between the hustle and bustle of life and the peace of the afterlife. But this morning she was too wired to appreciate it.

Since she always took the long way around to get her heart rate up, she arrived at Susan Locke's grave breathing heavily. The pitted coral stone wasn't large or imposing, but it always shocked her. *Her mother was dead.* She still couldn't believe it. Maybe because the ovarian cancer had taken her mother's life so quickly, though she had kept the knowledge and pain of the disease to herself for months, in much the same way she'd kept other aspects of her life secret.

Robyn looked around nervously then zeroed in on the Stargazer lilies she had placed by the grave last week, early on the morning of her wedding day. She preferred real flowers as the unrelenting sun and salt air turned the most beautiful artificial flowers into colorless and shredded heaps over time. The sight of the dead and droopy flowers brought back her grief with renewed power. She missed her mother, now more than ever. As wonderful as it had been to be reunited with the father she had fantasized about as long as she could remember, her relationship with Raul couldn't compete with her ties to her mother. Her mother had always been there. It was a simple as that.

With a start, she realized that she'd never told Raul about her weekly visits to her mother's grave, almost as if she was jealously guarding her special relationship from him. Not that he'd asked, which was surprising in itself. After all, she had a cache of twenty years worth of letters from him to her mother, all of them professing his undying love. But from the moment she had informed him of her mother's death, he had never once asked where she was buried. Which now, standing here in front of her headstone, seemed rather odd.

She fished the last living lily out of the vase, then glanced over at the huge Poinciana trees to the right of the section where her mother was buried. That's where Vince had said Will would meet her.

She looked about but saw no one, not even another jogger. Still holding the flower, she approached the trees. As she got closer, the hair on the back of her neck prickled and her stomach knotted in fear. Was coming here alone a mistake?

Halting, she peered into the deepening shadows and thick bushes. "Will," she whispered, her voice shaking.

She clenched her fists. "Will?" she squeaked again.

A rustle came from the right. Her heart jumped into her throat. A dark form stepped out from behind one of the blooming Poincianas. At first all she saw was gray sweat pants and a gray sweatshirt, the hood up and obscuring the wearer's hair and face. "W-Will?"

"Hey." The familiar voice arced through her like a bolt of lightening, zapping all her fears and doubts and leaving her weak with relief. As Will stepped out of the shadows into the dappled sunlight, he pushed back the hood and broke into the grin that had won her heart from day one.

He reached for her and pulled her close. Then he swung her around until her feet left the ground. "I was afraid you wouldn't come," he said, naked relief in his voice and on his face.

Giddy with happiness, she started to laugh. "How could I not come?" she demanded. "How could you think I wouldn't?"

Her feet touched the ground as he released her, but she was still flying. When he cradled her cheek with one hand, his touch set off a wave of longing that obliterated everything else. Without hesitation she raised her mouth for the kiss she didn't know how she'd lived without for the last few days.

The taste and the feel of his lips were just like she remembered, only better. She framed his face with her hands, deepening the kiss, hungry for the reassurance of his love and the truth of their relationship. The smell of his skin and roughness of his unshaven jaw under her fingers seemed more vivid, more intoxicating than it ever had before.

Whatever the reason for the assignation, it didn't matter any more. What mattered was that they were together, alone, for the first time in days. Able to touch and be touched, to revel in the closeness and physical intimacy that the law had denied them, surrounded by the quiet of the early morning.

Will dragged his lips to her throat, his electric touch setting off sparks wherever it went. He unzipped her jacket and tugged it down her shoulders, then raised the sports bra to free her breasts. The cool air rushed in, only to be replaced by the supple warmth of his hands cupping the undersides of her breasts, and kneading and pulling on the nipples already erect with desire. When he lowered his head and suckled first one nipple, then the other, she gasped and her knees buckled.

He grinned slightly, his mouth still on her breast, his eyes dark with lust. Raising his head, he cupped her bottom and pressed her against the hardness of his groin.

She wriggled against him, her yearning reaching a fever pitch. Her hands slid under his sweatpants to find his slick, naked muscular backside, but it wasn't enough. She wanted more. "Please, Will, now. Please."

He captured her mouth once more and backed her up against the trunk of one of the Poinciana trees. He easily tugged down her sweatpants and her panties, and slipped two fingers inside her, already wet with need. He moved in and out, his tongue mimicking the motion of his hand, and building the tension inside her to an unbearable level.

When he finally lifted her and thrust inside, she moaned with pleasure. Her thighs tightened around his bare hips, and she arched her back as he thrust and thrust again, driving her to ever-higher levels of excruciating pleasure. Her fingers dug into his back when a thrust harder and deeper than all the others catapulted her over the edge and into a shattering explosion of sensation. She shut her eyes and heard a stifled scream rip through the cemetery.

Robyn had no idea how long it took before she came down to earth. Will was still inside her, his big hands bracing her back, his damp forehead pressed against hers, his breathing ragged. Her legs still clasped his waist, while her fingers tangled in the hair that curled at the back of his neck.

She coasted on the last swells of contentment before finally opening her eyes. Will smiled at her, his blue eyes knowing. "A screamer," he whispered. "My Robyn's a screamer."

"That was me? Oh, God, no!" A flush raced up her neck as all her customary reserve returned. "What if someone heard us? What if –"

His lips, warm and pliant, cut her off. "No one heard us," he said. "If they did, too bad. I've got the answer I needed."

"The answer?" Robyn blinked. "The answer to what?"

His smile widened. "Now I know it's not true."

"What's not true?" A twinge of fear invaded her happy haze.

"That you want out of our marriage, Robyn. That you want a divorce."

CHAPTER ELEVEN

Robyn slid down Will's hips and to the ground. Her hands slipped from the back of his neck to his chest.

"Divorce? Who said I wanted to divorce you?"

The anguish on her face made Will wish he hadn't said anything. But it was too late now.

"Sergei," he said. He brushed a lock of her silky hair out of her face, and wrapped it around his finger. "You know Raul offered to pay for a new lawyer for me after Mark's accident?"

"Yes." Robyn nodded. "Sergei told me just before we went into the hospital." She lifted her chin. "I thought it was a very generous offer."

"Did he tell you the condition?"

Her brow furrowed. "What condition?"

Will grimaced. There was no way to soft pedal it. "Raul promised to pay all my legal expenses, but only if I agreed to an immediate divorce."

"I . . ." The golden flecks in Robyn's rich brown eyes glistened. She pressed her lips together. "I . . . that can't be."

The closeness and joy their lovemaking had brought Robyn started to melt away. She had put her father on a pedestal, and now her husband of a week was taking a sledgehammer to it. "Sergei said you knew about the condition."

He waited for her to deny it. Finally, after a long, strained moment, she did. "No. I didn't know." Her eyes clouded, another sign that she was drawing away, shutting out what she didn't want to hear.

"Maybe it wasn't Raul's idea at all," he mused. "Maybe it was just Sergei putting a spin on the offer for his own purposes."

Robyn slipped out of his arms and picked up the sweatpants and thong she had no memory of wriggling out of. As she dressed, he retied the drawstring on his sweat pants and struggled to find the right words to deliver even more unpleasant news. He should have told her long ago, when it first happened, but she'd been so thrilled with her newfound father that he hadn't wanted to burst her bubble. Now there was no choice. If their marriage was to survive, she had to know.

"There's something else."

"What?" It was only one word, but it had the harsh, strangled quality of a person close to tears.

He reached for her hand. To his relief, she didn't pull away. "It's about your father." He paused, then plowed ahead. "This isn't the first time he's tried to interfere in our relationship."

"If you're trying to tell me that he doesn't think you're good enough for me, I already know that."

"It's worse than that." He took a deep breath. "On Raul's second trip to Key West, he took me out for a drink." Just the memory made his stomach clench. "Your father explained, very politely and carefully, why I wouldn't make you a good husband. When I refused to step aside, he offered me money."

"Money?" The last of any color from their lovemaking drained from Robyn's face. "But . . . but he paid for our wedding. If he was so against it, why would he pay?" Her voice grew louder, belligerent. "That doesn't make sense."

"I don't know why. I just know that he did. And it didn't stop there."

Robyn flinched. "What . . . what do you mean?"

"You remember Raul and I arguing outside Saint Mary's just before the wedding?"

"Yes, but –"

"Raul tried to convince me to stand you up. He said he'd invest in Ryder Brother's Construction, pay off the house, everything, if I'd do the right thing and stand aside. He'd take care of you and your hurt feelings, as long as I took off."

"He wouldn't!"

"He did."

Robyn wrenched her hand from Will's. When he reached for her again, she backed away. "I've got to go. It's late. I'm supposed to be at –"

"I'm telling the truth, Robyn. You've got to believe me."

"How can I?" she cried. "How can I believe anyone?"

She turned and fled into the bright sunshine of Palm Avenue's exit to Passover Lane and the welcome release to her workday.

≈≈≈

A half hour later, Robyn stormed back into the house. She'd gone straight to work from the cemetery, only to realize she'd never be able to concentrate on anything as inconsequential as invoices and bill payment. No, she needed to confront Raul, to find out if the horrible things Will was saying were true, but in lieu of him, Sergei would have to do.

"Sergei," she called as she stomped through the house, but no one answered. Through the French doors off the dining room, she glimpsed a flash of pale skin and navy cloth against a lounger on the porch. Sergei.

She opened and shut the door behind her and opened her mouth to blast him. He was asleep, and on the table beside him sat a half-full mug of the strong black coffee he favored, as well as an ashtray containing a couple of cigarette butts.

She kicked the edge of the lounge. "Sergei!"

"Huh?" He blinked awake. His chiseled face blossomed into a smile. "You're back so soon."

"Never mind that. Why didn't you tell me about the condition?"

"Condition?"

She crossed her arms and tapped her fingers on her elbow. "The condition that Will agree to a divorce if Raul paid his legal expenses."

"Oh. That." Sergei yawned, sat up and swung his bare feet to the floor. He extracted a cigarette from the Belomorkanal pack on the table, lit it then took a long drag before squinting up at her. "Why are you so surprised? You know Raul has no use for your husband."

"Maybe not. But he could have at least told me. *You* could have told me!"

"Well, I didn't." He yawned again. "Besides, the offer was to Will, not to you. If he'd accepted it, then it would have proven Raul's point that Will's been after his money from the start."

"But he didn't accept it, did he?" Robyn snapped. She loved her father, and he'd been nothing but generous with his time and money. But if what Will said was true, her father had stepped way out of line. "And what about before? Outside the church?"

"What about it?"

"Is it true that Raul tried to buy Will off, to give him money if he stood me up at the altar?"

Sergei shrugged. He drew on his cigarette again; the pungent odor made Robyn wrinkle her nose. "How would I know? You didn't invite me to your wedding, remember?"

"And what about before that? Will said Raul tried to bribe him to break our engagement."

The Russian arched one eyebrow. "You've been talking to Will again?"

Robyn flushed. "He's my husband, Sergei. What do you think?"

Ignoring the last exchange, Sergei stood up and smiled grimly. "I don't know what kind of relationship you think I have with your father, but it's not that close. Yesterday, today, I'm here only as a favor to him. But the rest of it, I know nothing about. You've got Raul's cell number. Call him and ask."

"Maybe I will," Robyn said, knowing she wouldn't. Raul would be back in a couple of days. This kind of conversation should only be had face to face. In the meantime, there was something she could do.

"I want you to get your things and leave."

"Now?" The Russian gestured to the clear blue sky overhead. "It's a beautiful summer day. We could walk the beach, snorkel a little, maybe go out in the boat, do a little fishing. Put some color back into your pale face."

The tips of his fingers brushed her cheek, bringing with them the smell of nicotine. She recoiled. "I don't need my father – or you – to take care of me, thank you. And I doubt Will would like you going in his boat. Now get your things and leave."

He raised his hands in a gesture of pacification. "All right. I'll go. Raul isn't going to be happy about this though."

"But I will be" Robyn retorted.

≈≈≈

Once Sergei left, oozing both charm and regret, Robyn deflated like a punctured balloon. Shock, anger and indignation had propelled her home to confront Raul's associate, but now that she was alone, she started to sag under the weight of the doubts that refused to go away. She removed the ashtray and mug from the table, and collapsed onto the lounge Sergei had surrendered only minutes before.

Was Will telling the truth? Sergei had confirmed the odious condition Raul had set to provide money for Will's legal defense, but what about everything else? Would her father really have gone behind her back to buy Will off before the wedding?

To believe what Will said was to tarnish the image of the father she'd held in her heart since early childhood, an image she had embellished and polished in his twenty-six year's absence until he had taken on impossibly heroic dimensions. Dimensions, which to her delight, had held up well in the flesh. Raul had turned out to be not only a handsome, charming and rich mining executive, but also a loving father who in the last few months had showered her with the love and attention she'd craved for years.

But to <u>not</u> believe what Will said was to question everything about her relationship with him. Their physical relationship had sizzled right from the start, but what had finally made her agree to marry him ran far deeper than that. Over the weeks and months of seeing each other, she had slowly come to the conviction that Will was so much more than a pretty face and hot body; he was a good man. Honest, hard-working, fair, decent. Kind and gentle, not to mention fun to be with. Everything that Ralph Kleiner hadn't been. Everything that she wanted. Slowly her fears had receded until finally, if a bit shakily, she had agreed to make that second trip to the altar.

Is it possible that I'm wrong about Will too? Had all her caution, all her attempts to gauge his good and bad qualities and make a decision, been off base from the start? Was she every bit as blind and stupid as she'd been ten years ago when she'd run off with the high school football star?

She stared out at the slightly rippling waters of the Atlantic, deep turquoise against the cloudless sky. Two jet skis zoomed by, likely to be joined by more as the tourists became alive after a night of partying. In the past few days she'd discovered things about Will's past, about Vince, things that looked bad mostly because Will had omitted telling her in the first place. But did that mean he was trying to hide them? She remembered the look on his face when he'd seen the ransom money hidden in their linen closet. Was he capable of faking that much shock? Her stomach clenched. Was he capable of kidnapping her for money?

She shut her eyes. *No, no and more no!*

And yet her father, a self-made man who with his partner Eduardo De Guzman had built a mining empire, had disliked Will from the start. In the weeks before the wedding, the only objection to Will he had raised had concerned his ability to support her. But looking back, Robyn realized she'd known her father was more than a little contemptuous of Will. And if Will had disliked Raul, he had kept it to himself, just as he'd kept Raul's attempts to bribe him secret. But why? Why not tell her? Surely she should have known the truth.

If, indeed it was the truth.

Too jumpy to sit still, Robyn got up and went to the bedroom. From the second drawer of her Dade County Pine dresser, she retrieved the sheaf of letters she'd found amongst her mother's things after her death. There were twenty-three of them, tied up with plain string, and hidden in the back of her lingerie drawer. They were all from Raul; most of them dated in the first few years after he returned to Argentina, but the last one as recent as five years ago. And in all of them, Raul in one way or another, professed his love for his wife and daughter, and requested they return to his arms.

Finding the letters had been like discovering a treasure trove of information about her father. Susan Locke had been a very private person. While she lived, she said nothing bad about Raul, but neither had she satisfied her daughter's naturally curious questioning. Why didn't her father come to visit? Why had they divorced? Why didn't he ever phone or write to her? Did he love her?

The letters provided a window to the father Robyn had never known. She read each one dozens of times, lapping up the Spanish terms of endearment for her mother and herself, reveling in the information about his growing business and his new business partner. *Mi amor. Cara. Niña preciosa.* Her chest had tightened each time she read those phrases. It was because of the letters that ultimately she had contacted her father.

She removed the top three letters and left the rest on the dresser. These were her favorites, two from the early years, and the most recent one. They were the letters that spoke most directly to her heart, satisfying the need of the little girl she'd once been to know that somewhere out there she had a father who loved and cared about her. The last one always made her tear up.

Returning to the porch, she sat down on the lounge and unfolded the last letter. All of them had been written by fountain pen, and the thick blue script flowed smoothly across the yellowing linen paper. Her gaze went immediately to the final paragraph, one she had committed to memory.

So, mi amor, this is the last letter I shall ever write to you. I love you. I will always love you, but it is past time I accepted our marriage is finished. I had hoped, with the years, that you would find it in your heart to forgive me, but clearly that is not to be. Give my love to our daughter.

Robyn stared at the words that had moved her so often in the past few months. The father she'd come to know through these letters, the father she'd met in the flesh for the first time just a few short months ago, that man would not go behind her back to destroy her relationship with Will.

Yes, he wanted her to divorce Will. He'd made no secret of it, in fact had badgered her endlessly the night before he left for Denver. And Sergei had confirmed the condition he'd placed on what she'd thought was such a kind offer to Will. But none of this had happened until they'd found the ransom money in the house, and Will had been arrested. Raul had taken it not only as an assault on her, but an attack on him. It should come as no surprise now that he was pushing for divorce any way he could.

But before that? She didn't see it.

Any more than she could see Will lying to her.

The letter fell into her lap and she dropped her head into her hands. The current horror show of her life was starting to make her first marriage almost look good.

≈≈≈

As the police boat rounded the east side of Wisteria Island, Robyn shuddered. It was just a little further on and less than a week ago, that the kidnapper had dumped her into the open water.

And if Special Agent Rolland was to be believed, it was on this very island, so close to her home, that she'd been held captive for three days. Shortly after Sergei departed, the FBI agent had called with the news they'd discovered the hiding place. Did she want to see it? She'd accepted, less out of curiosity or a desire to help the police than a need to escape the doubts tormenting her in the silent house.

Robyn studied the shoreline. Except for another police boat anchored offshore, a dinghy pulled up between some bushes, and a flutter of yellow police tape, the overgrown hump of land looked as deserted as ever.

The driver killed the engine and dropped the anchor. He, Rolland and Robyn piled into a small dinghy and rowed towards a patch of sand and low-lying bushes a few yards away from where the first dinghy was pulled up on the beach.

The driver was the first to exit, his rubber boots sinking into the wet sand in the knee-deep water. Rolland jumped, his dress shoes landing with a squish in the soft ground. He cussed. A soaker for sure. Robyn took off her flip-flops and eased into the water. The sand oozed between her toes. "Ouch!"

"What was that?"

Robyn winced. "Just a rock." She looked down, but the sediment they'd stirred up obscured her view.

They pushed their way through the dense trees and bushes until they stood in front of a makeshift structure in the center of the island. It was in far worse shape than Robyn had anticipated. The rust-covered roof sagged. A few flakes of paint were all that remained of the dark green door. The windows were haphazardly boarded up with plywood.

"Who owns it?" she asked Rolland."

"Name's Clara Yundt. She's eighty-two and been in a retirement home for the last three months. She's unmarried, and from what we can figure out, hasn't been to it for at least fifteen years - probably left over from the shark camp days" He looked at her. "Have you ever been here? I mean before the kidnapping."

"No. Will and I –." She stumbled to a halt then forced herself to carry on. "We meant to, but never got around to it."

Rolland lifted the police tape. "After you."

Robyn scooted past him to the rickety steps to a tiny front stoop. He caught up and nodded at the flip-flops in her hand.

"You might want to put those back on. It's pretty dirty in there."

"I know. But I might recognize how it feels. My feet were bare the whole time I was . . ." She swallowed. "Held captive."

He shrugged. "Up to you."

Robyn slipped through the open door. Police had erected lights in either corner of the small front room. At the far end, directly across from the front door, was a wall and two more doors, one to the bedroom, the other to what had to be the bathroom. In the corner behind her were a small counter and a few poorly made frontless cupboards, and beside that the smallest oven she had ever seen. An oblong wooden table and two chairs were shoved against a dirty overstuffed chair and a love seat both of which had been home to more than one family of rats. An old broom, its few remaining strands curled and dirty, leaned against the chair.

She frowned. She'd thought she would know, immediately, if this were the place. But it wasn't so simple. She shut her eyes and took a deep breath. The smell was the same, the dusty, musty smell, though not as overpowering. Maybe because the door was propped open now, letting in fresh air.

She opened her eyes and walked to the bedroom. Her stomach heaved when she saw the thin bare mattress on the metal frame, the only furniture in the tiny room. Was this it? The room looked so small, so cell-like. She shuddered and moved closer, her gaze moving over the ripped and stained covering inch by inch. Was that a soup stain, from the tomato soup that had dribbled down her chin and onto her clothes?

She sucked in more of the stale air. Should she lie on the filthy mattress, see if it felt the way she remembered, smelled the way she remembered? Now that she was up close she was reluctant to touch it much less get her nose near it.

One of the techs angled a light into the room, increasing the illumination. The dust was more evident than ever, and more rodent droppings than she wanted to think about dotted the floor. She was about to turn and leave when she noticed a thread waving from the side of the metal frame.

She crouched down and reached under the bed.

"Hey, don't touch any–"

She yanked the thread free and stood up. She held it in front of the light. Her wedding dress had been custom made, and for months she'd looked at designs and fabric and thread samples, until finally she'd chosen, out of dozens of almost identical shades, a particular shade of ivory. French Crème, it was called. The exact shade of this strand of silk thread.

"This is mine." She turned around to find Rolland in her face.

"I told you not to touch anything."

"This thread is from my wedding dress," she said. "It must have caught on the bed frame when the kidnappers took it off me."

"You're sure?"

"Of course."

Rolland held out a gloved hand. "I'll take the thread, Mrs. Ryder. Please don't touch anything else."

For the next few minutes, Robyn wandered the cabin, mostly trying to keep out of the way of the people diligently searching and cataloging every inch of space.

Finally she'd had enough. She escaped outside, taking in huge gulps of the fresh air. Rolland joined her a moment later. "Seen enough?"

"Yes." She swallowed, suddenly feeling queasy. "That's the place. I'm sure of it."

He nodded. "Good. We'll take you home now."

Robyn reached the dinghy first. Pulling her denim Capri pants higher she waded into the warm water and gazed down to avoid sharp stones like the one that had stabbed her foot earlier.

A flash of red and gold caught her eye. She looked more closely. Visible through the ripples of the now clear water was the blond wood handle and diamond-shaped label of a Henry Taylor chisel – the chisel that she must have stepped on getting out of the boat.

And the same make of high quality chisel as the set she'd given to Will last Christmas!

Her stomach twisted. She pushed down on the chisel with her foot, burying it deeper in the shifting sand.

"Hurry up," she called to Rolland and the driver. "Let's get going."

CHAPTER TWELVE

"You really don't need to do this."

"Yes, I do." Mark Ryder grimaced as he shifted position on the hospital bed. His legs, swollen double their size and wrapped in removable fiberglass casts, stretched out in front of him on the hospital bed. Despite the morphine drip, Will could see that every movement, however small, cost his younger brother.

"Will is right." Dave Federenko nodded from his seat on the other side of the bed. The criminal lawyer's navy suit, close-cropped graying hair and neatly trimmed beard made him look older than his forty-two years, but his keen blue eyes missed nothing. He tapped the file in his lap. "I've got the limited information you have already. The rest I can get from Will and the prosecutor's office."

Mark wriggled again, producing another wince. "You're missing the point, guys. I *need* to help." He glared at Will. "Not only because you're my brother, but because it takes my mind off the pain. Okay? So let's get on with it."

That was fine with Will. It was Monday, three days since he'd been charged with kidnapping Robyn, and he felt as if he was mired in mud. Mark's accident had taken priority, but now it was time to get back to his own pressing concerns. Meeting Robyn yesterday morning at the cemetery had only made things worse. He'd known his accusations against her father would greatly shock her but he never expected her to run from him.

Dave opened the file then looked up. "What about you, Mark? Have the police got any leads on the hit-and-run driver?"

"They've found the SUV they think was involved, abandoned close to the Salt Ponds by the airport. It was a Mazda, reported stolen early Friday night."

Dave frowned. "Stolen, huh? You don't think it was kids then, out for a joy ride?"

Mark snorted, then immediately flinched. He looked at Will. "I can't laugh, either." He said wryly then turned to Dave. "I don't think most joy riders leave their lights off and go from zero to fifty in five seconds flat. Do you?"

"No." Dave glanced at Will, then back at Mark. "You got enemies you haven't told me about? An unhappy client?"

"Not unhappy enough to try to kill me. Because whoever hit me did it deliberately. There's no doubt in my mind."

Will absorbed the information in silence. Who would want to kill Mark? Who would −?

Suddenly he made a disturbing connection. *Could it be*? He leaned forward. "Friday at the jail − did you tell Robyn, or anyone else, that you weren't going to represent me?"

Mark paused. "I doubt it. And I'm sure I didn't tell her when I called her later. I didn't get a hold of Dave until after I drove you back to Dad's place."

"What about Raul Leopoldo?"

"No, not him either. No one except you and Dave."

Dave looked askance. "Raul Leopoldo? Isn't that your father-in-law? What does he have to do with this?"

"Nothing, probably." Will shrugged. "It's just that one of his business associates delivered an interesting proposition to me at the hospital Saturday morning."

"A proposition?" Mark asked. "What about?"

"Money." Will grunted at the memory. "Apparently my father-in-law – who, by the way, is convinced I'm both a kidnapper and a thief – was concerned that I wouldn't be able to afford a lawyer after you were mowed down. He offered to pay for a new one."

Mark grinned. "So why didn't you take him up on it? It would get the aunties off the hook."

"There was a condition." Will paused. "I had to agree to divorce Robyn."

Stunned silence met his comment. Dave tossed the file aside. "Let me get this straight. You're suggesting your father-in-law had someone run over Mark so he could try to force you to divorce his daughter?"

"Not exactly," Will said, though now that Dave had put it into words, it didn't sound as far-fetched as it should have. "I think he saw an opportunity to get me to do what he wanted, and he took it. He didn't think I was good enough for Robyn right from the start. But that's not what I'm getting at.

"No, what I'm saying is that Mark's hit-and-run and the kidnapping charges against me could be connected."

He looked from Mark to Dave. "Whoever set me up for the kidnapping may be the same person who ran down Mark."

≈≈≈

Robyn made no attempt to control the angry slap of her rainbow colored slides on the floor as she followed the hostess through the Cafe Marquesa in the Marquesa Hotel to a table by the window. She'd already waited four days for her father to return to the hotel so she could confront him about Will's accusations of bribery. The thought of waiting for three or four more hours was unbearable.

But wait she would. Raul had thwarted her need for an immediate one-on-one when he'd swept into Island Fit thirty minutes earlier, Sergei in tow, and announced with a flourish that he was celebrating his return by taking she and Izzie out for a much deserved elegant dinner. Izzie had jumped on the invitation and Robyn had bottled up her frustrations and pasted a tight smile on her face.

She took a window seat and busied herself unfurling her napkin. With all the doubts, the questions, the worries swirling around in her head, how was she going to survive dinner and small talk? Her head already felt as if it was going to explode. Had Agent Rolland or the sheriff's deputies found the chisel in the mud at the island? Was it Will's? If it was, how had it gotten there? Had Raul really tried to buy Will off? And if he hadn't, why was Will lying?

As Raul sat beside her, and Sergei and Izzie slid into the seats across from her, she grabbed a menu and hid behind it. She glanced out the window. Tourists and locals were making their way to their favorite watering holes and restaurants. Her stomach clenched and the pounding in her head grew worse. *Why did I agree to come here?* The exact place, even the same table, where Will had proposed to her so many months ago.

Fighting back the sting of tears, she forced herself to study the gourmet menu. Raul's bare elbow jostled hers.

"It's lovely here," he said. She knew he was smiling at her, but she didn't look up.

"You know," he continued, "if you are not going to expand your health club, you should consider opening a small restaurant right in the club parking lot. With your location, and the great views to the outside world, it would attract tourists with ease."

"That's a terrific idea," Izzie chirped. "We could have lots of glass and a French or Cuban menu. Cappuccino, espresso coffees for the members, maybe a discount too. We could . . .

Izzie's excitement grated on Robyn's strung-out nerves and aching head. She loved her friend's bubbly personality, but since Will's arrest, Izzie had been a little too effervescent. She'd gone out of her way to be helpful and to relieve Robyn of any unnecessary work, but she'd also gone out of her way to report every shred of gossip. Did Robyn know that John Ryder had a moonshine still in the cistern under the house when the brothers were kids? That Will had been suspended from his football team one semester for drinking underage? About the speeding tickets, the drag races on Hwy 1, blah, blah, blah? The rumors that Mark used his law degree as a front to launder money for his clients?

Robyn gritted her teeth at the memory of the nasty rumors. She'd finally told Izzie to shut up. If and when she changed her mind about Will, it wouldn't be because of gossip.

Now, with a gigantic effort, she composed herself and lowered the menu. Sergei, seated across from her, gazed out the window for a long moment then smiled over at her. "This reminds me of one of my favorite places at home."

The smile, a little wistful, struck just the right note. Robyn grasped at the straw of neutral conversation he offered. "Where's home?" she asked.

"Moskva – Moscow." He gestured to the window. "This view makes me think of the tourists walking to Saint Basil's Cathedral in Red Square. I loved to go there as a child. I still do."

He leaned in close to Robyn his voice lowered so only she could hear. "Perhaps one day you will join me in a boat cruise down the Moscow River?"

He sat back, his smile widening and his left cheek dimpling in a way she'd never noticed before. "But of course, as much as I love Moscow, I hope soon to make my home in your beautiful United States. There is so much opportunity, so much deal making. And so many beautiful women."

He winked, and for once his open flirtation didn't annoy her. It was better than listening to Izzie run the Ryders into the ground. Or Raul browbeating her into getting a divorce.

"You've never said. How did you come to work with Raul in the first place?" she asked.

"We met at a mining conference in Argentina. We were both interested in expanding internationally, particularly investing in resource companies based in America. Your father already had dual citizenship, which with his experience and investment funds, gives him an entree I lack, but which I hope soon to rectify."

Their drinks had arrived and he raised his shot glass of vodka. "To America, the land of opportunity."

She clinked her iced tea against his glass. Given what she'd read about the difficulties of life in Russia today, even for a well-heeled businessman, she could understand why he might want to live elsewhere.

Izzie and Raul joined in the toast, raising their sweating water glasses too. Raul drank and then set his glass on the table and smiled at Robyn. "As for me, I am happy to have the opportunity to freely visit my beautiful daughter, and provide whatever support and guidance I can to make her life easier."

Robyn smiled stiffly and picked up her menu again. On the surface, Raul's comment sounded gracious but, from the experience of the last few days, she knew it was likely a prelude to another "divorce that bastard Will" lecture, something she couldn't face right this minute. "The Diver Sea Scallops are really incredible," she said from behind her menu.

The waitress took their orders and Robyn lost her menu shield. She tried to look interested as Izzie started rattling on about the jump in interest in Island Fit membership in the last few days.

"It's got to be the notoriety," she said, rolling her eyes. "We just don't have anything this unusual happen around here. You don't know how many people have come in asking if this is the club owned by the lady who was kidnapped by her husband. They ask all the girls to point Robyn out."

Robyn snapped up out of her seat. Tomorrow, at work, Izzie was going to get a blast. How could she be so insensitive? But for now, a couple of Advil would have to do. "I'm going to the washroom. I'll be right back."

Raul and Sergei stood as she slipped out from the table. She left the dining area, and headed to the women's washroom. She had just reached the door when a voice stopped her.

"Robyn!"

The head and shoulders of a white-capped member of the kitchen staff stuck out from the doorway Robyn had passed two seconds earlier. At first she didn't recognize the pale, make-up-free face below the baker's hat. Then it hit her.

Laura Rennick. Her ex-employee. The one who had lured her out of the tent to be kidnapped. The employee – the friend! – who had betrayed her by stealing from a member, not just once, but twice?

Her headache surged to head-splitting proportions. *No bloody way!* She whirled away.

"Please. I only want a moment. Please."

The desperate, plaintive tone of Laura's voice reached her through the pounding pain. She hesitated then slowly turned, her body stiff. "Why should I give you even a second? You stole from me. The police don't think so, but you're probably responsible for my kidnapping too!"

Laura stepped around the doors and they swung shut behind her. In the crisp white uniform, with her white-blonde hair tucked up inside her cap, her narrow face looked thin and wan, except for the red blotches on her cheeks. Tears shone in her hazel eyes.

"Please," she whispered. "I'm so sorry about what happened. I had no idea when I sent in that note that someone was waiting to grab you."

Robyn put a hand to her pounding temples. "So you say."

Her hand dropped to her side and she glared at the former friend. "What I really don't understand is how you could steal from the club members. You've worked there almost from the beginning. You're supposed to be my friend. It's not as if you weren't well paid."

"I didn't steal!"

Robyn sniffed. "Then how did that wallet get into your pocket?"

"I don't know. I swear it." Laura wrung her hands, and the red blotches spread down her neck. "I never go into the members' change rooms. And I wouldn't steal."

Laura's distress seemed real, but Robyn hardened her heart. "Come off it. Izzie says it's not the first time, either."

"What?" Laura froze.

"She says it's not the first time you've stolen," Robyn said impatiently.

"That's not true!"

"No? Then why would she say it?"

"Because . . ." Laura looked over her shoulder. "Because I saw Izzie kissing your father in the office that morning."

CHAPTER THIRTEEN

Laura's words screeched through Robyn's headache like fingernails on slate.

"What?" she finally managed. "Is this some kind of sick joke? You think –"

"No!" Laura reached for her arm. Robyn backed away until her backside hit the washroom door.

"Please, come through the kitchen with me. I'll tell you everything."

Robyn hesitated. Should she tell Laura to take her lies and buzz off? She looked at her former friend's face. If she was lying, she was doing an incredible job of acting.

"All right. But only for a moment."

Laura led the way through the kitchen to the door to the outside. She turned to face Robyn.

"It happened early the day of your wedding rehearsal. You took the day off, remember? I came in at six fifteen, a half hour earlier than I was supposed to. I had a training session with a guy I hadn't seen in several months, and I wanted to go over his records before we got started. The blinds were drawn in your office, but the door was open an inch or two, so I just pushed it open. And there were Izzie and your Dad, in a clinch."

Robyn frowned. "You're sure it was Raul?"

"Yes. You introduced him to me when he first came here."

"Did they see you?"

Laura nodded. "Yes, they jumped apart. I mumbled something about records and coming back in five minutes, and backed out. When I came back, your Dad was gone, and Izzie was working at her computer."

"Did she say anything?"

"No, she ignored me. I assumed she was embarrassed, so I didn't mention it either."

Robyn rubbed her forehead. It was hard to think with the boot stomping tattoo in her head. The thought of Izzie and Raul together was weird, but why not? Izzie had been moaning her lack of a boyfriend for months now, and her father, though in his mid-fifties, was an attractive and vital man. But why would Izzie feel the need to hide it from her? Raul, she could understand. While he'd been hungry for all the details of her life, all the things he had missed, he'd given short shrift to many of her questions. From the first meeting, he'd struck her as an intensely private man who kept his feelings to himself. That was one of the reasons she valued his letters to her mother so highly.

"So you think Izzie found a pretext to fire you because you saw them together?"

"I don't know." Laura wrapped her arms around her middle. "All I know is I saw them together in the morning, then in the afternoon I was accused of stealing Ida Moran's wallet. Izzie said if I went quietly, she wouldn't call the police, and she'd tell you I resigned."

"And what about the other incident? When you stole before?"

Laura's lips pressed together so hard a white line formed around them. "There was no other incident. I never stole anything. Not at your club."

Robyn frowned. *"Not at your club?* What's that supposed to mean? That you stole from other people you worked for?"

Laura's face flamed; she looked as if she were about to burst into tears. But she didn't answer the question. "Please believe me," she begged, her voice cracking. " After all this time, you can't think I'd steal from the members. Please tell me you believe me."

Robyn cringed. She'd heard those words too many times already in the last few days. She dropped her head into her hands and turned away.

"Believe you? How can I believe you? How can I believe anyone?"

≈≈≈

"No, I want the bike on the landing, halfway up the staircase!"

The two men delivering the heavy stationary bike to Island Fit Thursday morning didn't even try to hide their irritation. The smaller of the two, a wiry man in his mid-thirties, stuck his hands on his hips. He nodded over his shoulder to the open stairs. "Are you sure, lady? No one can use it there."

"Of course not," Robyn snapped. Barely eight a.m., and she'd already had it with people questioning her judgment. Her father. Izzie. The police. Laura. "The bike is for display only. It's a prize for bringing in new members. I want it where everyone can see it."

Muttering under their breaths, the two men heaved the bike up from the table where they'd set it, and zigzagged across the floor to the steps. They finally maneuvered it up the first flight of stairs and positioned it on the narrow display table wedged against the waist-high side of the open landing.

Robyn signed the delivery papers and the men left. She stood back and looked up at the gleaming new bike on its heavy base. It was a top-of-the-line exercise machine. Sitting on the stand on the open landing, it could be seen from the fitness class area, the weight-machines, the aerobic and cross-trainers, as well as the front desk and the lounge area near the front doors. Once it was strung with ribbons and the red and white banner announcing the contest was hung from the landing, the prize would be the center of attention for the month-long-promotion. A similar campaign last year had brought in one hundred and twenty curious visitors.

"D'you think that's the safest place for it?" Izzie came and stood by Robyn's side. "It could get knocked over the wall."

Robyn clenched her fists. Did everyone think she was stupid? "It's as solid as the ones sitting on the floor," she said evenly. "Even if you fell against it, it wouldn't topple; the base is too heavy. But if you're that concerned, we can rope it to the handrails."

Izzie blushed. "Okay. Look, I'm sorry, hon. I know I've been on your case a lot the last few days."

"Yeah." Robyn turned and looked at her pointedly. "You have been. A lot."

"Oh." Izzie sucked in her breath.

Now that she'd started, Robyn decided to continue on the offensive. The air needed to be cleared on more than one subject. "There's something I need to talk to you about. In the office."

She headed to the door, Izzie trailing behind her. Once they were inside, she shut the door.

Izzie started talking immediately. "I know I've been harsh. I really don't think Will had anything to do with your abduction, no matter how it looks or what the gossips say."

"Good." Robyn leaned against the edge of her desk and crossed her arms. "But you wouldn't know it from your behavior. And I don't appreciate your using it as a marketing opportunity either."

Izzie's pink face burned a dull red. She started twisting a lock of frizzy hair that had escaped her ponytail, and looked down at the floor. "I guess that was going a bit far. But you know how things are today. Like it or not, you're sort of a celebrity."

"That is so twisted!" Robyn sniffed. "But that's not what I want to talk to you about."

Despite her headache last night, in the privacy of his hotel room after dinner, she had confronted Raul about Will's accusations. To her shock, he had not only admitted trying to buy Will off, but had proudly defended his actions. "And I was right, too," he insisted. "The kidnapping proves that all Will Ryder was after from the start was money – your money, my money. All I was doing was protecting you, my dear daughter. I only wish I had been successful."

Infuriated, Robyn had denounced his interference in her life. "I can take care of myself," she had repeated. "I can make my own decisions." Though she was unable to wring an apology from him, eventually he had agreed to stop bad-mouthing Will and stop badgering her for a divorce. Now it was time to get down to the bottom of what Laura had said about him and Izzie.

She raised her chin and looked directly at her friend. "No, what I want to talk about is you . . . and my father. And the fact that you're dating."

"What?" The red zoomed back into Izzie's face. She looked as if she'd swallowed a goldfish. "I . . . no, we're not!"

"Hmm. That's funny. Because I ran into Laura – you know, Laura Rennick – on my way to the washroom at the Marquesa last night. She works there now, in the kitchen. She told me that she interrupted you and Raul kissing, right here in this office, the day before my wedding. She also seems to think that's why you fired her."

"That's not true!"

Robyn sighed. She lowered her hands to the desk. *Laura's exact words last night.* "Which part isn't true?" she asked quietly. "That you're seeing Raul, or that it's the reason you fired Laura?"

"Neither . . . I . . ." Izzie stuttered to a halt.

"Come on, Izzie. We've known each other for ten years. You've always supported me; you always seemed to love Will. Now, all of a sudden, you're down on him. Raul's down on him too." Robyn paused. "It's not a coincidence, is it?"

"No . . . oh, all right." Izzie conceded defeat. "Yes, I've been seeing Raul. We started seeing each other just a few weeks before your wedding."

She clasped her hands together and her bottom lip jutted out. "But it has nothing – absolutely nothing – to do with Laura getting sacked. She stole. That's the only reason I got rid of her."

Robyn refused to commit, at least not yet. "Why didn't you tell me? About you and Raul? Why hide it?"

Izzie snorted. "Oh, yes. You're always so fair-minded." She plopped into her chair. "Think about what you're saying, Robyn. Raul is your father. You've only had him around for a short time. Are you ready to share him with someone else? I mean, he is your father, not to mention old enough to be my father, too. I thought you'd be annoyed."

"Annoyed?" Robyn thought about that for a minute. "I don't think so. It's a little weird – my best friend and my father – but annoying, no." She studied her friend. "Actually, I can see why you might be attracted to each other. Raul is a vital, charming man, and you're so bubbly and gorgeous."

Izzie smiled glumly. "You mean fat, don't you?"

"No, I don't mean fat! I've always thought you were amazing, in every way, Izzie, far more beautiful than some of the stick-like women who come in here."

"All right." Izzie cut her off. "But you won't tell Raul I told you?"

"Why not?"

She worried her full lower lip quivering. "You know how private your father is, and how much he likes everything his own way. Raul was very insistent we not tell you about us until everything is cleared up with Will and the kidnapping. He wanted to wait until things were all right for you before he gave you the news."

"News?" Robyn raised an eyebrow. "What news?"

Izzie grinned. "That I'm going to be your new step-mother!"

≈≈≈

At six forty-five Friday morning, Will called Vince's cell. Vince was fifteen minutes late picking him up from their father's house for the commute to a work site on Cudjoe Key. They were building a garage, one of the few jobs that hadn't been cancelled after the kidnapping charges were laid, and Will didn't want to lose this one too.

After four rings, voice mail kicked in. Will paced the porch of his father's house. "Ah, come on," he muttered after the beep. "Pick up, Vince. Or wake up, if you're not up yet. We're going to be late."

Five minutes later he tried again. He hung up when the voice mail clicked on. Five more minutes went by. He called again. The same result.

His father came out of the house. "Still no Vince?"

Will shook his head.

John Ryder threw him the keys to the ancient Jeep sitting in the drive. "Drop me off at work and you go on to Vince's. See what's up. It's not like Vince to be late like this."

They drove in silence to the Conch Tour Train Roundhouse on Flagler in Midtown where the elder Ryder worked as a Conch train driver. Will's father took the phone, and tried to raise Vince a couple more times, with no success. When he got out, he dropped the cell on the passenger seat. "Give that brother of yours a kick in the butt for me."

"Will do." Will smiled tightly. His father might joke, but they both knew Vince never drank more than a beer or two. He didn't smoke or take any mind-altering drugs either. No, his only addiction had been gambling; the one-armed bandits in the casinos in Miami that had sucked up all his money and led to his dismissal from the Key West Police Department. But he hadn't been near a slot machine since he'd started working with Will, and he'd never been late either.

Twenty minutes later Will pulled into the Poinciana Mobile Home Park, a small but well-kept trailer park not far from him down the street. Six months ago Vince had bought a used trailer, and had been living there ever since. It was quite a change from the house in Midtown he'd lost along with his job, but he seemed to be happy there. He liked his neighbors and in the last few weeks had often mentioned the single mother – Lynda, wasn't it - who had just moved in next door.

As he turned onto the road to Vince's, he saw the Ryder Brother's panel truck parked in its usual place. Could Vince's budding relationship with his new neighbor have jumped to a new level? Perhaps he'd overslept, but in another bed? Except there was no car parked beside the neighbor's trailer and it looked deserted.

Will got out of the Jeep, climbed the two steps to Vince's porch, opened the screen door and banged on the inner door. There was no answer, so he tried the door. It was locked.

"Vince!" He pounded on the door a few more times. Nothing. If Vince was asleep, he was really out.

Will jumped off the porch and made his way to the back of the trailer and the bedroom where Vince slept. He grabbed a couple of cement blocks abandoned in the long grass near the next home, piled them up and stood on them to look in the window. The navy mini-blind was drawn, but a few of the slats were twisted and open. He cupped his hands around his eyes and peered through the small openings.

It took a few seconds for his eyes to adjust. The only light came from the trailer's living room, through the open bedroom door, and the few bent slats. Once adjusted, his gaze traveled to the computer monitor on Vince's desk. The computer was on but in hibernation mode; only the time in block letters was swirling about on the screen.

Will's gaze moved lower, and then froze. Slumped over the arm of the chair was a man in a white t-shirt, his arm and head hanging lifelessly towards the floor. Dark spatters covered the shirt, and a dark pool spread along the floor from the side of the chair and a blue pillow he liked to prop his legs up on after standing on them all day working.

Will jumped off the blocks and pulled out his cell. As he ran for the door, he jabbed in 911.

The dispatcher came on the line at the same instant that his booted foot kicked open the door.

"My brother's been shot," he shouted into the phone as he ran through the living room. "I need an ambulance and the police at the Poinciana Mobile Home Park.

Now!"

CHAPTER FOURTEEN

Three days later

"No, dearie, I'm afraid Will can't see you right now."

"But I just want –"

"Dear!" Marcy, the middle sister of the three tiny aunts, straightened to her full height of four foot ten. The old woman's eyes shone with sympathy, but her tone was as steely as the blue of her short permed hair. "We both know that's not a good idea. There's the court order, of course, but –"

"But what?"

"Will isn't up to seeing anyone right now. You can understand that dear, can't you? I mean, after your kidnapping, his arrest, Mark's accident, and now Vince." She started to pull the screen door shut.

"Yes," Robyn said as she caught the door with her hand. She could understand what Will and his family was going through. Which was exactly why she was standing on John Ryder's front porch begging entry. She didn't know how much comfort her presence would be, but she had to try. Especially since the media were suggesting Vince's death was suicide.

Marcy tugged on the door to shut it but Robyn didn't release her hold. "Okay . . . what about John, then? Could I at least speak to him for a moment or two? Give him my condolences?"

Marcy sighed. "You're a darlin' Robyn, and I've already passed your sympathies to Will and John. But they're both so raw right now . . . they just can't see anyone. I'm sure that will change in a few days. Maybe after the funeral."

"The funeral?" Robyn started. "When is it?"

"Goodbye, dear." Marcy pulled the door free from Robyn's now slack fingers and shut it, then the inside door.

Robyn blinked at the closed door. Being shut out from Will when he was hurting so badly was not only unbelievable, it was unbearable. Will wouldn't answer her calls. The ancient auntie brigade had arrived at the first word of Vince's death and they'd provided better security than the best of trained guard dogs.

She rubbed her head as the tightening in her temples heralded a new headache. She still couldn't accept that Vince was dead. When the news had arrived late Monday morning, she and Izzie had clung together in shock, until Izzie had broken down in sobs and run for the washroom. A half-hour later, when she emerged, red-eyed and red-nosed from sobbing, Robyn had sent her home. She'd wanted to go too, but had waited, fruitlessly it turned out, at the club for Will to call her.

When she finally got home, the tragic news had silenced even Raul and Sergei. There were no more diatribes against the worthless Ryders or efforts to get her started on divorce proceedings. Her father especially, crept around her Monday and Tuesday evening as if she were fragile glass about to shatter. She'd been relieved when they both left for Argentina this morning. But even with their departure she hadn't been able to get to Will.

Her hand fell to her side. With a heavy heart, she turned and thumped down the stairs and along the sidewalk to her silver Beetle. It wasn't until she'd slammed shut the door and turned the key in the ignition, that a plan came to her.

Mark! Mark was still in the hospital. He was in a private room. Maybe he would accept her sympathy. Maybe he would give her some straight answers.

She squealed away from the curb. Would Will know that was her? That at least she'd tried to see him? That she cared?

Ten minutes later she was running through the main doors of the Lower Keys Medical Center. As she approached his room, she realized she didn't have a clue what she was going to say.

She stopped in the open doorway. Will's younger brother, who looked so much like him, lay on his back, his legs splayed out in the fiberglass casts like two blue painted boards. His eyes were shut, and on the bedside table was a neatly folded copy of yesterday's *Key West Citizen*. Even from the doorway, Robyn could see the glaring mega font of the front-page headline she couldn't forget: *Kidnapping suspect's brother shot dead.*

She took a deep breath. She didn't like to wake Mark, but she had to know what was going on. "Mark?"

"Robyn." His quiet response was immediate, making her suspect he'd known she was there from the second she arrived. He turned his head, his eyes mere slits in his gaunt face.

Shock rippled through her. Mark looked far worse than he had immediately after the hit-and-run and the operation to set his legs. She crossed to the bed and took his hand. "I'm so sorry about Vince." She struggled to keep her voice from breaking. "It's just . . . I still can't believe . . ."

Mark's weary gaze held hers a beat too long, and for that one moment, she imagined it was Will's hand she was holding. Then he looked away. "Believe what? That he's dead or that he committed suicide?"

His bitterness shook her. Mark had always been the sunny one, Vince the dark and brooding one, while Will staked out the middle ground. "I can't believe either of them," she said. "May I sit down?"

She pulled a vinyl-covered chair up to the bed and sat down, her hands now in her lap. "I'm so sorry," she repeated. "Vince was so good to me, especially these last few days since Will's arrest."

"Yeah."

It was evident Mark didn't want to talk to anyone, maybe least of all her, but she wasn't giving up. "I don't want to pump you for information, but no one else will tell me anything, and I need to know."

She paused. "Was there really a suicide note? That's what the media reports are saying?"

"Of sorts." Only Mark's lips moved.

She frowned. "Of sorts?"

"It's complicated."

She leaned forward. "I've got time to listen. Even if that's all I can do. All right?"

At his faint nod, she continued. "You don't really think he killed himself, do you?"

Mark's eyes shut. Finally he sighed. "My contacts in Sheriff's Office tell me all the evidence points that way. Vince's .32 caliber ankle gun that was his back up pistol when he was on the force was found on the floor with his prints on it. The angle of bullet entry to the head is compatible with a self-inflicted wound. To make matters worse, the cops found evidence in his trailer that he'd started gambling again. They found receipts for cash advances from the Seminole Casino in Hollywood.Robyn gaped. "Vince was gambling again? I don't believe it."

"That's what we all thought." Mark's eyes flicked open and he grabbed the controller for his bed. Accompanied by a low buzz, the top of his bed moved upright until he was in a semi-sitting position. "But people can be really good at hiding addictions. I've learned that from some of my own clients. Dave Federenko – that's Will's new lawyer – has got a P.I. looking into it now."

"Dave Federenko." Robyn repeated the name. So much had happened in the last week that she hadn't found out what Will had done after turning down Raul's insulting offer. "Do you know . . . does Will need help paying his legal fees?"

Mark smiled mirthlessly. "The auntie brigade," he said. "They're taking care of it."

"Good." She was happy the aunts were helping Will financially, but not okay with them keeping her away from him.

"What about the note?" she asked. "Did Vince say why he wanted to die?"

Mark stilled. "Actually, the note was more of a confession."

"A confession? A confession to what?"

For a long time Mark said nothing.

Gently she prodded him. "Mark?"

He raised his head slightly off the pillow and looked at her, his blue eyes dull with pain. "A confession that he and Will planned your kidnapping to get money to pay his gambling debts."

≈≈≈

Robyn had never crashed a funeral before. But she'd genuinely liked Vince and not being able to offer her sympathies and comfort to Will and his family had pushed her beyond caring what was "best" for everyone and into the realm of desperation. She was going to the funeral, whether anyone liked it or not.

The moment she stepped inside the small, somber room and caught sight of the remaining Ryders, gathered like a black cloud around the plain casket, she knew she'd done the right thing. Vince's death, following so much violence, had wreaked heartbreaking changes on the Ryder clan. John Ryder, her father-in-law, had visibly shrunk and aged in the last few days, a change made all the more dramatic by the black suit that hung listlessly on his hunched form. Mark's sunny humor had evaporated, replaced by a bitter visage and clenched fists. His girlfriend Sam, holding the wheelchair in place, lovingly squeezed his shoulder but he didn't seem to notice.

The change in Will was worst of all. In a black suit, shirt and tie, he stood silent and immobile behind his father. His tanned face was gray, his jaw set, his blue eyes hard and unreadable, and his arms hung straight and stiff at his side. Whatever sorrow he had felt had been shoved aside by something far more violent. He looked as if one spark, one wrong word, would set off an explosion. The only sign that he'd seen her was a slight flicker of his eyes before he turned away.

A ring of pain tightened around Robyn's heart. Will needed her now but there was nothing she could do about it. She sat in the last row of chairs set up before the coffin. Like two blackbirds, the two youngest of Will's aunts perched in the second row. Marcy turned and frowned at her. This second recent drive from Miami to Key West and for such a horrible reason had put a significant strain on their attitude towards her. In front of Robyn sat two men in dark suits, probably friends of Vince's from his days on the Key West PD. There were a few other people she barely recognized, cousins and other relatives she'd met at the reception.

A moment later the minister arrived, a short, round, balding man Robyn had never seen before. Fidgeting with his metal-framed glasses, the minister led a brief service, consisting of prayers, a mournful rendition of Amazing Grace and two other off-key hymns sung by a middle-aged woman who accompanied herself on a small organ. The aunts discreetly blew their noses and wiped at tears with lace hankies. No sound came from the front row of Ryders, though John Ryder's rounded shoulders shook with silent sobs.

To Robyn's surprise, Will rose and came to the podium. After a nod to the minister, he looked out at the small group, his expression grim although some of his anger seemed to have dissipated. Under normal circumstances it would have been Mark, the lawyer accustomed to public speaking, who gave the eulogy.

Will didn't waste any time on jokes or stories from Vince's life. His message was blunt, and as raw and forceful as the emotions raging through all the Ryders right now.

"Usually eulogies celebrate the life of the person who has died. In Vince's case, there's a lot to celebrate. We all have memories of his kindness, his decency, his strength and humor. But those stories are going to have to wait for another day. Because Vince, like all of us, had frailties, and at times, they got the better of him. Vince's frailty was gambling and, unfortunately, it appears that he had started to gamble again. My biggest regret – the regret of everyone in our family – is that none of us noticed the signs. If we had, we might have been able to help him fight off this particular demon."

Will swallowed; Robyn knew this was a sure sign he was fighting to control himself. His fingers loosened and tightened repeatedly on the edges of the podium, then he started again.

"Vince's gambling aside, I am serving notice that none of us – not Dad, Mark or I, not Aunt Marcy or Aunt Peggy – believe Vince took his life. Gambling aside, Vince was a strong man. He'd faced his demons in the past. We know he could have --*would* have -- faced them again.

"Nor do we believe he wrote the note confessing to the abduction of my wife and naming me as his accomplice. Vince loved Robyn like a sister. He would never have risked hurting her, especially for money."

Once again Will halted. He took a deep breath to center himself. When he spoke again, his voice was much lower.

"And Vince loved me. He was the older brother who looked out for me, and whom I looked up to for as far back as I can remember. It's because of him I didn't get into more trouble as a teenager. He was a force for good. He would never have led me into crime, especially crime against my own wife."

For a second, Will's determined gaze met Robyn's, and the strength of his conviction burned into her. "Finally, I am serving notice, that we – Mark, my father and I – will do everything in our power to find Vince's murderer."

Robyn started. One of the aunts gasped. Will's lips thinned. "That's right, murderer. One way or another, we will find Vince's murderer, and see that he or she pays for taking his life and framing him for a crime he didn't commit. Vince is dead. Mark has two broken legs. I'm charged with kidnapping. For Vince's sake, for all our sakes, the Ryders aren't going to take any more."

He left the podium and sat down. No one in the room spoke. Robyn was stunned, but prouder of Will than ever.

Because Will was right. Vince was innocent, just as Will was innocent. Deep inside, she'd known it from the start, but had let circumstantial evidence, her father's prejudices, and her own insecurities shake her faith in him. Her doubts had been a reflection of her mistrust of her own judgment, rather than a judgment of the man she loved. Unfortunately, it had taken Vince's death to make her see the truth.

The organ music started up again. The minister took the podium for the benediction.

Robyn was out of her seat the moment the minister stepped down. She had already wasted far too much time. She wasn't about to waste a second more.

Will stood with his back to her. She tapped him on the shoulder. Before he'd completely turned around, she flung herself at him. As she hugged him, she mumbled into the side of his neck. "I'm so sorry about Vince." Once she'd started, the words came tumbling out. "So sorry about Mark. So sorry I doubted you, even for a moment."

As she eased away, his arms slowly moved around her. His blue eyes, shadowed with pain and hesitation, searched hers.

She took both his hands. Her gaze held his, trying to show him by word and manner what had been there all along, locked deep inside. "I know you're both innocent. I know Vince didn't kill himself. And I know that you love me."

The harsh line of his jaw softened as his resistance began to melt. She wrapped her arms around him again and whispered so only he could hear.

"I miss you. I'm alone at the house tonight. Come over at midnight."

≈≈≈

At twelve minutes after midnight, the crunch of gravel outside sent Robyn running to the window. She parted the blinds and peered out, just in time to see lights doused as the garage door closed behind a dark vehicle. It had to be Will, didn't it? Raul and Sergei were in Argentina. It could only be Will.

178

She shivered as she crept to the hallway that led to the door across from the garage. On impulse, she picked up a ten-pound kettlebell she'd brought home from work.

The key turned in the lock, and the door swung open. Will's lean form filled the doorway. She exhaled sharply. Thank God!

She relaxed and let the kettlebell fall to her side. Will's gaze followed the movement then returned to her face. "You planning to use that on me?"

She cleared her throat. "No. I was nervous, that's all. I'm not good at this sneaking around."

She started to turn away when his warm hand closed around her upper arm. "Don't be sorry. After being kidnapped, I wouldn't be surprised if you came to the door with a gun."

He followed her down the hallway. She deposited the kettlebell on the floor and continued to the living room.

"I put Dad's Jeep in the garage."

The sound of his low, husky voice sent shivers of another kind along her spine. Now that he was finally here, she felt awkward. Once she reached the living room, she turned to face him. "Good. I don't want anyone guessing you're here. I'd hate you to end up back in jail."

He smiled then, but it didn't reach his eyes. "So would I."

The awkward tension grew. Like two nervous teenagers on their first date, they stood several feet apart not quite looking at each other. At last, Robyn gestured to the sofa and two glasses of sparkling wine sitting on the coffee table. "Sit down and have a drink."

"Champagne?" He raised one eyebrow as he sat down and reached for a glass.

She flushed. "Sparkling wine. It's not to celebrate. Only to . . . to help us relax. That's all."

She sat down a couple of feet away from him on the sofa, grabbed the remaining glass and took a gulp. For the first time since he arrived, she truly looked at him. It was Will all right, the man she'd married a mere two weeks ago. But at the same time it wasn't. Everything was the same, but yet different.

Gone was the easygoing optimism and good humor, even the innocence that had been a part of his personality, incinerated by the horrors of the last two weeks. What remained was a guarded, somber man who expected the worst. Deep shadows darkened the once bright laughing eyes, eyes she no longer felt able to read. The lines around his eyes and his mouth had become more pronounced and spoke of a hardness that had not been there before. While he was only two feet away, he seemed distant, remote.

And her lack of belief was at least partially to blame. Yes, her abduction, his arrest, Mark's accident, and now Vince's death had all dealt full body blows. But her failure to trust him had been the final twist of the knife, the one he had never expected.

She struggled to make amends. "I'm sorry. About everything." Her voice caught. "Especially about not believing you . . . Raul admitted he tried to buy you off."

He set down his glass. "You don't have to apologize."

"Yes, I do. I should have –"

"No." His sharp denial cut her off. That and a renewed brightness in his blue eyes. "I understand why you couldn't trust me one hundred per cent."

"What?" Robyn sat back. "How?"

He leaned over and placed her hands between both of his, the pressure warm and reassuring. His long fingers, the pads roughened from work, trailed across her palm and along her wrist simultaneously awakening and soothing her senses. A tingle of excitement ran up her arms. He looked down at their joined hands for a moment, then back up at her.

"Because I felt exactly the same way about Vince when I saw that note confessing that he and I had kidnapped you."

CHAPTER FIFTEEN

"**W**hat? What are you talking about?"

His jaw relaxed and the hardness in his eyes softened. "Because I know how it feels to have the rug pulled out from under you. To be faced with something – in this case Vince's alleged suicide and confession – that's makes you feel as if you never knew the person at all. That makes you doubt everything about him."

He paused. "Just like you wondered about me after you found the ransom money in our closet."

"I didn't –"

"Yes, you did." His hands tightened on hers and he began slowing caressing them. "And I'm not blaming you. I'm telling you that I understand." He leaned towards her. "I'm just glad you came around."

Robyn couldn't drag her gaze away from the mesmerizing pull of this man she both knew and didn't know. "How – how did you make the leap to what you said this afternoon at the funeral? To believing that Vince was murdered, and that the confession note was fake?"

Will moved closer, his bare arm against hers, his denim-covered thigh rubbing ever so slightly against her bare leg. "Once I got past the shock, I realized it was impossible. Yeah, we didn't know about the gambling – and I won't believe that until I see more proof – but even if it's true, it doesn't matter."

His blue eyes darkened; he'd never looked stronger or more determined. "Because I know Vince. Mark knows him. So do Dad, and Sam, and you. There is just no way he would have done any of these things. God knows he wasn't perfect. He got kicked off the police force. But he was a good man, with a good heart. He . . ."

His voice broke and he turned away. Gently Robyn framed his face with her hands and brought him back. "He was a good man," she said quietly. "Just as you're a good man."

For a long moment their gazes locked. He seemed to be searching for something, his eyes plumbing the depths of her soul, looking for proof she meant what she said.

Robyn didn't hesitate. She leaned forward and kissed him tenderly. She wanted to infuse each kiss, each touch, with all the comfort and love she had for him, to show him by action what she had failed at so miserably with words. To make up, somehow, for her lack of trust. To love him until he knew without question she would never doubt him again.

But the moment her lips brushed his, her fingers tangled in his hair and slid across the back of his strong neck, her need for him took over. What was supposed to be gentle and tender suddenly grew urgent. What was supposed to be all about him, suddenly got confused with all about them. His unique taste and the pliancy of his lips and tongue fueled her hunger, setting off fires that raged through her veins and burned like an inferno in her belly. She needed bare skin against bare skin, mouth against mouth, his hardness against her softness, and she needed it now. Slow and tender would have to wait.

Driven by their increasingly heated kisses, she attacked the clasp and zipper of his jeans while he pulled the camisole over her head. He shimmied out of his jeans and boxers and yanked off his t-shirt, while she dropped her flirty pink polka dot boy shorts and kicked them to the other side of the room.

He lay back on the sofa, his eyes gleaming with a hunger even the room's shadows couldn't hide. Even if a glance hadn't told her he was more than ready and waiting for her, his words dispelled any doubt. "Come here and take me," he growled.

She wasted no time straddling his narrow hips. She lowered her head to capture his lips once more and he cupped her breasts, his roughened fingers caressing the soft mounds and creating increasingly sharp waves of pleasure. She tightened her thighs around him, moving faster and harder against him as their kisses grew deeper and more demanding.

Finally his hands slid down her hips to cup her buttocks, and lift her over him. When he entered her, it felt so unbelievably good that she couldn't help grinning. When he grinned back, her naked form reflected in his shining eyes, her heart soared. Everything was going to be right between them again! "Now," he commanded.

She didn't need to be asked again. She started riding him, slowly at first, then more quickly, until both were moving at a frantic pace, driven on by the rising sensations and desires neither could deny. Her breathing ragged, her back arched, she intently watched the face that she loved. When he finally groaned and flung back his head, his climax sparked her own body and soul-wrenching response.

She collapsed against him, nestling her head in the space between his head and his shoulder. He held her close and for the first time in weeks, she felt whole again. She lapped up the closeness, the scent and feel of him, trying to store it all in her memory to keep her going during the trying weeks and months that lay ahead.

Finally he brushed his lips across her forehead. "Thank you."

"Thank you?" She rose to look at him. "For what?"

"For trusting me again. You don't know how much that means to me."

Robyn's throat tightened. Tears stung her eyes. "I –"

He touched his fingers to her lips. His eyes, dark with tenderness, met hers.

"It's all right, Robyn. I love you. You love me. Somehow – I don't know how – but somehow we'll get through this together."

≈≈≈

Sometime during the next few hours, Will and Robyn moved into the bedroom and onto the bed, with its freshly laundered sheets and turned back quilt. They made love long and slow, hard and fast, and everything in between, and still it wasn't enough.

The illuminated numbers of the bedside clock said three fifty-eight and Will knew he had to leave before light. He disengaged from Robyn's sleepy embrace and swung his feet to the floor. When he returned a moment later, zipping up his jeans, Robyn was wrapping a short silk robe around her waist.

She looked up and the heat of her gaze almost had him shucking his jeans once more and tossing her onto the bed for more of the same. But time was short, and they had to talk.

He fastened his jeans and sat on the side of the bed. Reluctantly he broached the painful topics. "We need to talk about Vince's death and that confession note, as well as your abduction," he said. "If they're connected – and I think they are – then whoever is orchestrating this attack is far more dangerous than any of us realized."

He tried not to be distracted by Robyn's swollen lips, the wavy hair his fingers had tousled only moments before, the   nipples poking against the thin silk fabric of her robe. He wanted to take her in his arms again, but if he did, he'd never get around to saying what had to be said.

Robyn nodded. "Do the police really think Vince killed himself?"

Will flinched. The pain of Vince's death was still too sharp to ignore. He swallowed. "Whatever the police think, they're not telling me. But I've heard through my lawyer, and through Mark, that the police are uneasy with this whole thing. Everything is too pat, too neat. Even if they believe Vince and I arranged your kidnapping, they still don't have a clue who did the actual act. Obviously, neither Vince nor I could have done it."

Robyn flushed. "There's something I did the other day that I probably shouldn't have. When Agent Rolland took me to the island and the cabin where they think I was held, I – I saw something."

"Yeah?"

"It looked like one of the chisels I gave you for Christmas. It was half-buried in the sand in the water where we pulled up the boat. I was so startled I shoved it deeper into the sand."

At first Will was shocked. Robyn had doubted him enough to hide evidence? Then he relaxed. "You shouldn't have done that," he agreed. "It might not even be mine, but if it is, it actually supports the theory that I'm being set up. Even Rolland would have to wonder why I'd be stupid enough to leave one of my tools at the scene of the crime."

"D'you think I should tell him now?"

Will shrugged. "It can't make things any worse than they already are."

Her face still flushed, Robyn changed the subject. "But who could have done it? Who would have killed Vince?"

"It's got to be someone who has it in for me and my family. Someone attacking us from every side – kidnapping you, planting the ransom money in our house, the ransom notes, even undercutting Ryder Brother's to get our contracts."

"The contracts?"

"My lawyer Dave Federenko has got a P.I. looking into that too. Some out-of-town outfit came in and undercut our estimates at the last minute. In each case the clients were ready to go for us, but the deal they were offered was so good they couldn't pass." He paused. "So good I don't see how they could have made a profit on the job."

Robyn played with the belt of her robe. Will struggled to resist pulling the belt loose and exposing the lean body beneath.

"What about Laura Rennick?" she asked. "Izzie fired her the day before the wedding because she stole a club member's wallet. I can't see her going this far for revenge, especially not killing Vince, but she is the one who sent the note just before I was kidnapped."

She yanked at the belt. "And then there's Ralph. I went to see him after your arrest. "Mostly it was a waste of time, Ralph just being his usual nasty self. Except he did mention something odd. Something about a silent partner, and how he didn't need money from me any more."

Will nodded. "The question is, is Ralph twisted enough – or crazy enough – to take out his frustrations on you and me. And just as importantly, would anyone with a brain trust him as a partner in anything?"

Will paused. So far Robyn had been with him every step of the way. She was going to balk at what he said next, but it had to be said.

"What about Sergei Kakovka?" he asked slowly, his gaze fixed on her face. "He's made no secret of his interest in you. Could he have something to do with this, or your kidnapping at least?"

To Will's surprise, Robyn nodded. "It's possible, but unlikely. He's come on to me several times, especially when he's had too much to drink. But to set up a conspiracy to blame you for my kidnapping? Run over Mark? To kill Vince?" She shook her head. "Unless we're living in some kind of parallel universe, I don't see it."

Will took a deep breath. She'd definitely not like his next conjecture. "What about your father?"

He raised a hand. "No, no hear me out. I don't want to think Raul has anything to do with your kidnapping, my arrest or Vince's death, but I can't discount him. Not when he's tried to buy me away from you at least three times.

He, if no one else, has the financial means to have arranged everything that's happened."

The angry denial he expected didn't materialize. Instead she sighed and looked down at the silk tie now a mass of knots.

"I can see why you might think Raul was a suspect. But I know him better than you do. Despite all his rages, all his harangues to divorce you, I can't see him doing it. He's very old world, and takes his role as my father very seriously. A lot of what you're seeing is his frustration that he hasn't had a larger part in my life and that I won't obey him just because he's my father. But I'm sure he had nothing to do with the abduction or Vince's murder, and I can show you why."

She went to her dresser, opened the second drawer and removed a bundle of papers. It wasn't until she sat down again that Will saw they were letters, folded and bound with a ribbon. Robyn removed the top few letters, and set the rest down beside her.

"I found these letters in my mother's things after she died. They're from Raul, letters he wrote over a twenty-year-period to my mother. I'd never seen them before, but in every one he writes about how much he loves her and me, and begs her to come back to him. It's because of the letters that I know he could never have done anything to harm you or me."

She handed the three top letters to Will. "These are the three I like best. Read them. And then tell me that you think Raul is a killer and a kidnapper."

Will took the letters. Robyn got up and left the room to go make coffee. He read first one, then another. The emotion in each one surprised him, as did the yearning, spoken and unspoken, that pervaded each line. It was evident in every word that Raul was suffering because of the separation from his wife and daughter, and that he would give anything to get them back. The letters were strong and vivid, but they also made Will uncomfortable, as if he were a peeping tom looking through a stranger's windows.

But there was something else about the letters that made him uncomfortable, something he couldn't quite put his finger on. Before he could figure it out, Robyn returned. "You've finished reading the letters?"

He nodded.

"So you can see why I don't think it's possible my father is behind the kidnapping or Vince's murder?"

"Yes," he conceded. From the moment he'd met Robyn, he'd known that she yearned for the father she'd never had. When she found Raul, she'd idealized him, and the letters certainly bolstered the image of a loving, devoted father. But did they convince him? He wasn't so sure.

"All right then." Robyn smiled, taking his lack of comment as agreement. "Now we just need to decide which one of us is going to look into Laura, Sergei and Ralph."

Will rose and drew Robyn to him for a last embrace. Robyn's faith in him had revived his hopes and his spirits.

He only wished he could share her faith in her father.

CHAPTER SIXTEEN

The sun burned through the thin and wispy Cirrus clouds early Monday morning as Robyn tied the laces on her running shoes and set off through the gates of the Key West Cemetery. Now that she had vanquished her doubts about Will, now that they had a plan to get to the bottom of her abduction and Vince's death, she was invigorated. It wasn't going to be easy, but she knew they would do it. And they would do it together.

As her feet pounded out a steady rhythm, she cleared her mind and gave herself up to the intense endorphins of running, the smell of the morning air and the increasing sounds of crowing roosters. She reveled in the feel of the ground beneath her feet, the strength and sureness of her own limbs over the uneven terrain of the grassy paths and the quiet historical beauty that surrounded her on every side.

In the distance, a worker on a mini tractor pulled a cart full of tools, the only sign of human life. So when she finally came into sight of her mother's headstone, she was shocked to see someone already standing there.

It was a man, his back to her. Could it be Raul? But he wouldn't be back until later this week.

Her jog slowed to a walk. As she got closer, she recognized the bent shoulders in the light jacket and the silver bowed head. It was George.

She slipped her hand through his arm. "Good morning, George. I didn't expect to find you here this early."

She looked over at his face. The tracks of tears glistened on his grizzled cheeks.

"Oh, George." She moved closer. "Are you all right?"

He wiped his face with the back of his hand. "I'm fine. As fine as a stupid old man who can't let go of the past can be."

"Don't say that!" she remonstrated gently. "There's nothing stupid about admitting you're still grieving for my mother. What do you think I'm doing here?"

Their eyes met. Her voice softened. "You know, sometimes I miss her more now than I did at first."

George attempted a half-hearted smile. "I can't stop wishing that we'd gotten married. Oh, I know it wouldn't have changed anything. She'd still be dead. But I can't help feeling we missed so much."

"Why didn't you? Get married, that is?" Robyn had wondered from the moment she'd been old enough to realize they were more than business partners, more than good friends. But while they'd worked together at Finnegan's, and spent most of their off-hours together, her mother had always maintained her own home. When Robyn had asked why, her mother had put her off, much as she did whenever Robyn tried to pry information about her biological father from her. Susan Locke had been a secretive person.

George shook his head. "It wasn't for lack of asking. I asked her every year from the time you were eight. The answer was always the same. No."

"Did she say why?"

"At first she said it was too soon after her divorce, you were too young, she liked her independence, that kind of thing. But after a while I realized it was none of those things."

Robyn frowned. "What, then?"

His gray eyes clouded. "Raul," he said simply.

"You mean my mother still loved him?" Robyn's eye's widened. While her mother had never said a bad word about Raul, she'd never let on she carried a torch for him either.

"No. That's not it. If anything, Susan was extremely bitter towards Raul. I was always amazed at the restraint she showed whenever you wanted to talk about him."

"Why was she so bitter? I know they got divorced, but all she'd ever tell me was that they didn't get along. It wasn't until I found those letters from Raul in her dresser that I realized there was something else. He kept apologizing and begging her forgiveness, but he never actually said for what."

George screwed up his face. "Well," he said, "I guess you have the right to know. I didn't see any reason to tell you when Raul showed up, because I thought you two needed to work out a relationship on your own, in the present."

"Tell me, please." Now that her own marriage was threatened, it seemed terribly important to understand what had driven her parents apart.

He sighed. "You know your mother grew up in San Diego? Well, she met Raul shortly after he'd emigrated from Argentina. He was smart, charming, well educated and they were married in a matter of weeks. He was a financial advisor, investing in businesses and stocks around the world, but particularly in South America. And he was very persuasive.

"He convinced Susan's mother and her brother to put most of their savings into a couple of startup ventures in Argentina. Not just them, literally all their friends and acquaintances. At first things were great, but then the investments faltered and eventually crashed. Raul lost everything. He declared bankruptcy. He wanted to take you and your mother and return to Argentina, but your mother refused. She insisted on staying and working to pay back the investors, particularly her family.

"So Raul left. Your mother stayed, but she couldn't face her family, so she moved across the country to Florida, and eventually Key West. She started working as a waitress at Finnegan's, and sent money back to her mother and brother every chance she could. It wasn't much, but she was determined to pay back every cent.

"Eventually Raul got back on his feet. When you were ten, he sent your mother a large amount of money. But it was too late. Her mother – your grandmother – had already died, and her brother had been killed in a car accident only weeks before. So she used the money to buy half of Finnegan's."

George sighed again. "I hate to tell you this, my girl, but your mother never really trusted anyone again after what happened with Raul. She loved me, I know. But she didn't trust me, certainly not enough to marry me. Even in the business, she made sure our partnership agreement left nothing to chance."

"Oh . . . I'm so sorry." George, of anyone in the world, deserved better. But something else he said had spiked her attention. "Raul – did he defraud all those people? My grandmother and uncle?"

"Oh, no." George stepped back. "Don't think I was trying to say Raul was a thief. It was nothing like that. Probably had more to do with youthful cockiness and not enough experience to back it up. It really was a case of picking risky investments and making inflated promises to the investors. If he'd been lucky, the investments would have paid off big time. Instead they tanked, and took everyone down with them.

"No, in your mother's eyes, the big problem was all the money lost by her family and friends. And the fact that Raul ran away rather than paying them back. That crushed her, changed her forever. She never forgave him."

"Oh, George." Robyn kissed his unshaven cheek then took his arm once more. "Where are you parked? I'll walk you back."

As they headed to the main gate Robyn's thoughts turned to her mother and the circumstances that had set her against Raul.   When push had turned to shove, when their world was falling down around them, Raul had deserted his wife and daughter for the safety of Argentina.

In the intervening years, he had grown up, become successful and paid off his debts. He had spent years begging her mother's forgiveness, and never getting it.

But had he really changed? Was he the loving and generous father he now portrayed? Certainly he had stepped over the line when he went behind her back to try to break up her relationship with Will. She'd attributed it to an overzealous concern for his only daughter. But what if she was wrong?

What if Will was right to suspect him?

≈ ≈ ≈

Everything had seemed possible after Will and Robyn's reunion in the early hours of Saturday morning. His spirits lifted by their lovemaking and Robyn's renewed faith in him, Will had left convinced it was only a matter of time before they proved his innocence and uncovered Vince's killer.

Reality was proving less promising. The first blow came late Monday afternoon when Mark took a call from Dave Federenko. Mark was back at his own place now, with several hours of home nursing provided per day. His secretary came by in the morning to do what work they could by phone and email, and Will had arrived at two p.m. Sam would be there after work. Will had rented a van and some tools this morning because the police now had Vince's truck too. But the truth was there wasn't much work to do since the kidnapping charges against him and Vince's alleged suicide. Instead, with assistance from Mark, he was using Sam's laptop to do a Google search on Sergei and Raul.

Mark clicked off the portable phone. He grimaced.

"Bad news?" asked Will.

"It's not good news. That was Federenko. The P.I. he hired says Vince visited the Seminole casino in Hollywood a half dozen times in the last two months. Alone, apparently."

Will swore. So Vince *had* started gambling again.

Mark continued. "The P.I. is still trying to track down exactly how much money Vince lost. Federenko will let us know as soon as he has anything."

For a moment, grief overwhelmed Will. Why hadn't Vince talked to him? Why hadn't he told him he was having trouble staying away from the slots? Had he been so engrossed in work and wedding plans that he'd missed his brother's calls for help?

The grief and shock quickly turned to determination. Because even if Vince had started to gamble again, that's no reason to kill himself. He wouldn't have kidnapped Robyn. And he certainly wouldn't have written a confession that implicated his brother in a plot he had nothing to do with.

Will retrieved Mark's laptop from the kitchen and deposited it on his lap. Sam had rented a hospital bed for Mark's recovery, and Mark and the bed now took up center stage in the living room.

"Why don't you find out as much as you can about Sergei, while I concentrate on Raul? It's Sergei Kakovka. K-a-k-o-v-k-a. All right? Robyn says he's from somewhere around Moscow. He's in the mining industry, just like Raul."

Mark nodded and set to work. Will returned to the desk and Sam's laptop. He didn't like to delve into Raul's life behind Robyn's back.

But he had to do it. No matter what she thought of her father, no matter what his letters seemed to say, Will couldn't let his suspicions go until he investigated further. Not with Vince dead. Not with Mark working from a hospital bed. Not with charges of kidnapping hanging over his own head. His expression grim, he typed "Raul Leopoldo" into the search engine.

For the next two hours, he tracked down numerous references to Robyn's father. "If only I'd paid more attention to Spanish at school," he groused as he scanned yet another all but incomprehensible reference.

"Yeah, and if only I could read Russian," responded Mark. "If only there weren't so many Sergei Kakovkas in the world."

Eventually Will found several articles about Raul in English on South American online newspapers and magazines sites. In one particularly long story from 2003, the writer described Raul as a "dynamic Argentinean businessman" whose perseverance and dedication had seen him through two early bankruptcies to unprecedented success in mining. After he partnered with Eduardo De Guzman, the two men had cut a swath through South America, convincing investors in Argentina and around the world to pursue their dreams of success in natural resources.

The article talked about Leopoldo and De Guzman's accomplishments, but also about their problems. Some of their employees had, indeed, been kidnapped, and except for one case where a Canadian geologist was shot dead, they had negotiated settlements with the kidnappers for undisclosed amounts. Nowhere did the article mention an ex-wife or daughter, or any family at all. It went on to say Raul Leopoldo was an extremely private man, whose preference was to be alone at his ranch in Cordoba, Argentina.

The company website, with Spanish and English versions, provided limited financial information about the company and a list of locations for Leopoldo and De Guzman-owned mines and ventures. Raul was listed as President and CEO, De Guzman the CFO. At the bottom of the home page was a link to something called LDG Worldwide Services.

But nothing, here or in any of the articles suggested that Raul, or the company, had engaged in any criminal activity, anytime, anywhere.

"Well, look at this," Mark interrupted.

Will got up and stood beside the bed. Mark angled his computer so Will could see the web page. Under a *St. Petersburg Times* headline was a small color photo that looked a lot like Sergei Kakovka. Above it was a headline that read, 'Big money in security for Westerners'.

"Apparently our boy has made millions providing security to western firms doing business in Russia since the fall of communism," said Mark. "His company and several others."

Will frowned. "I thought he was in mining. That's what Robyn said."

"Or maybe he just wants to invest some of those millions he's made through security contracts," suggested Mark. "Or provide security for mining operations in dangerous parts of the world."

"Maybe." Will said unconvinced.

"That's not all." Mark scrolled down to the bottom of the page. "You're not going to believe this.

"Sergei used to be a cop. A cop with the criminal investigations directorate in Moscow."

≈≈≈

The husky sound of Will's voice over the phone line set off a wave of longing so deep and strong Robyn shuddered. Though she was in her office with the door closed and the blind drawn, she glanced around guiltily. Anyone who saw her now would know without a doubt she was talking to Will.

"I miss you so much," she whispered. This court-ordered separation sucks, big time.

"Me, too," he said slowly, his voice thick with yearning.

After a moment of silence while she listened to his breathing like a giddy preteen, he continued. "You making any headway?"

Robyn paused. "Not yet. Izzie called in sick so I haven't been able to leave the club all day. I'm off shortly, so I'm going to stop by her place to see how she is, then try to raise Ralph."

"Are you sure you should see him alone? Maybe you could take one of your male personal trainers with you?"

"I'll be fine, Will." Robyn's heart warmed at his concern. "Never mind that. Have you found out anything about Vince or Sergei?"

He filled her in on what they had learned about Vince's return to gambling. Every reluctant word telegraphed Will's sorrow. She wanted to drop the phone and run to him, but that just wasn't possible.

"And then there's Sergei," he concluded. "We got another surprise there."

"What?"

There was a pause. "Did you know he used to be a cop?"

"A cop?"

"Yeah. And he doesn't work in mining. It's security services to western companies operating in Russia."

"Oh." Disappointment rose in Robyn's throat. "I guess that's one more suspect biting the dust."

"That's what I thought at first, but maybe not. According to the stories Mark found on the web, Sergei left the Moscow Police in the middle of a government investigation into corruption in the force. Several of his colleagues were charged with extortion, accepting bribes, that kind of thing, but he seems to have come out of it unblemished. Whether that means he's innocent, or just lucky, is difficult to tell. Mark's trying to follow it up."

Another pregnant pause followed. Robyn suspected Will had also discovered something about her father, something he wasn't telling her.

The awkward pause lengthened. There was so much to say, so much to do, none of it really possible in a phone call that wasn't supposed to be happening.

"I've got to go," Robyn said finally. "Can I call you at Mark's again tomorrow?"

Smiling, he said, "Better not. My brother the lawyer is already giving me the evil eye. But don't worry. We'll figure something out."

The call over, Robyn tidied up the office, gave last-minute instructions to Candice and Jake who were manning the desk for the evening shift, and headed out. She picked up food for two at the China Garden downtown before heading back to the cute little Conch cottage Izzie rented in Old Town.

Her worry about Izzie had skyrocketed after she'd called in this morning and said she was sick and wasn't coming in. She hadn't said sick with what, but Robyn could guess. Every day since Vince's death, Izzie had gotten tenser, more upset. She snapped at everyone, had burst into tears over a late delivery of water bottles, and had gone home early complaining of a headache on at least two occasions. The day of the funeral, she had vomited in the bathroom.

Maybe Vince was only a guy Izzie had dated for a few months and then dumped, but his death had hit her hard. It didn't help that Raul had been away when she needed him; in any event, he would have been unlikely to offer comfort for the death of any relation of Will's, especially one who had dated Izzie.

When Robyn pulled onto Angela, she noticed a For Sale sign on a house across the street and farther down from Izzie's. The Conch cottage was similar in size and style to Izzie's, but there the similarity ended. Dark gold paint peeled off the cracked and broken wooden siding. Poinciana flowers and pods covered the visible side of the rusted Victorian shingled tin roof, the porch railing had jagged gaps, and yellow Lantana obscured the stone walk to the door.

Robyn pulled into a narrow paved drive right behind Izzie's jeep. As she always did when she saw her friend's house, she smiled. Izzie had certainly lucked out when she rented the Shotgun house. With its creamy yellow shiplap siding, aqua shutters and gingerbread trim, it looked like a home right out of Coastal Living. And the inside was brand new, with a small but ultra modern kitchen, beautiful ash floors and white painted moldings, and a bathroom to die for. How convenient for Izzie that the professional couple who'd renovated it had been almost immediately transferred to Arizona.

Robyn grabbed the bag of takeout, the General Tso's chicken aroma making her stomach growl, and headed for the small front porch. As she climbed the two steps, she blinked in surprise. The last time she'd been here, the porch had been surrounded by a well-kept riot of purplish-blue Mexican Bluebells. Now the plants, instead of being trimmed and controlled were overgrown and so thick they were invading the front walk.

Robyn frowned. This wasn't like Izzie. She loved her plants, the way other people might love a cat or a dog. Had the events of the last weeks stressed her out far more than she was letting on?

She rang the doorbell and waited. Nothing. She rang again then tried the doorknob. Usually Izzie kept it unlocked when she was home during the day. Not this time.

Robyn set the bag on the porch, and pulled her cell out of the pocket of her shorts. She had just pressed Izzie's number on speed dial when the inner door swung open.

She looked up and saw Izzie. Her eyes widened in horror.

"What happened to you?"

CHAPTER SEVENTEEN

Izzie looked as if someone had hit her in the face with a shovel. Her left eye was swollen shut and bruised an ugly shade of deep purple. Beneath it, scrapes and bruises ran all the way down her plump cheek to her jaw. A jagged, painful-looking cut sliced from the corner of her mouth, and the left side of her full lips looked larger and more tender than the other.

"Pretty awful, isn't it?" Izzie croaked.

Robyn cringed. She stuffed the cell back in her pocket. "What happened?" she repeated.

Izzie's snort of derision turned into a wince of pain. She cleared her throat. "I know this sounds lame, but I tripped. Come in and I'll show you."

Forgetting all about the takeout, Robyn opened the screen door and stepped inside the Saltillo tiled entrance. Izzie stepped back and pointed to the marble threshold in the open doorway between the hall and the open concept living and dining area. The threshold stood about three-quarters of an inch higher than either the tiled floor or the hardwood on the other side.

"I meant to have that cut down when I moved in," Izzie said. "At first I was always stubbing my toe on it, and it really hurt. But I got used to it, and never did it any more. So I let it go.

"Until last night." She shook her head and winced again. "For some reason I hit it full tilt. And this time, I didn't just stub my toe. I went flying."

She pointed to a footstool in front of a wingback chair. The stool was covered with a quilted pad with palm trees, but each of the four corners was held up by a mahogany leg crowned with a decorative pineapple knob the size of a golf ball.

"My face smashed into the footstool. I'm not sure where or how I hit. I passed out for a moment or two. But when I came to, my eye had started to swell and my mouth really hurt too."

She touched her left upper arm, where another mottled bruise the size of a hand had blossomed. "I've got aches and bruises everywhere. And I think I've broken my big toe."

"Oh, Izzie." Robyn shuddered. She reached out to hug her friend, but Izzie stepped back.

"No, don't touch me. It hurts everywhere. But at least you can see why I didn't want to come in to work today. I look like someone took a baseball bat to me."

Robyn nodded uneasily. That's exactly what it did look like.

She glanced around the sparsely furnished but cozy living room. On the white sofa whose wooden legs matched the footstool, was a bag of ice covered in a dishtowel. "Oh, good. You've been icing it. Have you been to the doctor?"

"No." Izzie shook her head. "I'm not going out as long as I look like this. I know what the doctor will say, especially about my toe, and it doesn't matter. I've got painkillers. I've got ice. That's all I need."

"What about food? Are you hungry?"

"I was hoping you'd say that." Izzie looked back towards the door. "Do I smell General Tso's Chicken? My mouth is sore, but I'm sure I can still eat food in small pieces. Especially Chinese."

Robyn smiled. "Good." She retrieved the bag of food and started for the kitchen. "Where do you want to eat?"

"I wouldn't mind sitting on the porch. I look a fright, but I'll put on sunglasses and no one will notice. It's beautiful out there, especially in the evening."

Robyn went into the kitchen and unloaded the chicken and Vegetable Lo Mein onto two plates. She poured the Egg Drop Soup into mugs, got cutlery and headed for the door. Izzie, wearing wraparound sunglasses, hobbled behind her with the two mugs of soup. They settled themselves into lawn chairs.

They ate in companionable silence. Izzie, despite her injuries, ate everything on her plate and drained the mug of soup. When she finished her soup, she set the mug down on the small table between them.

"How are Will and Mark taking Vince's death?" she asked abruptly. "Poor Mr. Ryder. First Will's arrest, then Mark's accident, and now this."

Her voice wobbled on the last word. The sunglasses hid her eyes but Robyn suspected she was crying again.

"They're as okay as can be expected." Robyn looked out at the street. "Will has a new lawyer and he's helping them look into the kidnapping and Vince's murder."

"Murder?" Izzie gasped. "You think it's murder? The TV said it was suicide."

Robyn grimaced. While it wasn't official yet, she'd forgotten that Vince's death had been reported as a likely suicide. She took a deep breath.

"I know what the authorities say. I know it looks like suicide. But you knew Vince fairly well. Do you really think he would have killed himself?"

For a moment Izzie said nothing. Then she stood up, taking her mug with her. "I don't know. You want more soup? I'm getting some."

While Izzie limped inside for the soup, Robyn looked down the street at the house for sale. Besides being rundown, it looked deserted, as if no one had lived there for a long time.

Izzie returned and settled into the chair.

Robyn nodded to the house. "Who's moving?"

"Old Lady Yundt. She's been in the nursing home on Stock Island the last few months. One of her sisters has power of attorney and just put the place up for sale."

The name sounded familiar to Robyn. "Do you know her well?"

"No. She lived in Miami with her sisters but asked me over for tea when I first moved in. She wasn't good even then. I remember she served me moldy muffins."

Izzie shuddered. "After that, I used to go over when they were visiting. Sometimes I'd ring the doorbell and no one would answer, but I could hear the television blaring inside. She was the most deaf of all of them." Suddenly the dots connected and Robyn knew where she'd heard that name before. She leaned towards Izzie. "Yundt," she said. "Clara Yundt, right?"

"That's right."

"She's the one who owns the old shark processing plant where the kidnappers kept me. You know, the one where Special Agent Rolland took me last week. It's got to be her."

Excitement set Robyn's pulse racing. "I wonder . . ."

"Wonder what?"

"Maybe someone on this street is behind my abduction. Maybe it's someone Clara Yundt knows, or who knows her, at least well enough to know about the old camp. Did she ever mention a shark camp on Wisteria to you?"

Izzie snorted, then immediately flinched. She raised a hand to her head and her tone turned wistful. "You're so lucky to have your own home on the water."

Guilt welled up in Robyn. This was hardly the time to be pressing Izzie about her neighbors and what they might or might not have done. An idea leapt into her head, one she should have thought of the moment Will was arrested.

"Hey, Izzie. Why don't you come stay with me for the rest of the summer? I'm all alone, and I'd love to have you."

≈≈≈

Izzie resisted Robyn's pleas to get her to pack up her things and come home with her tonight. The best Robyn could extract from her friend was a promise to "think about it" once she was feeling better. And an assurance she'd stay home from work for at least a couple more days to recover.

But Robyn did come away with at least one potentially useful bit of information – that Clara Yundt's was now on Stock Island. Izzie had pooh-poohed the idea the old woman would be able to tell her anything useful – "she's got dementia, you know" – but it was worth a try. It was still early enough to visit Ralph Kleiner at the store. Since he lived in the back, it didn't really matter what time she went to see him, but daylight and going in through the front door was preferable to knocking at the back door in the alley that serviced that row of businesses.

She couldn't shake the idea that somehow her ex was involved in her abduction, if not Vince's murder. It wasn't that she thought Ralph had the initiative to pull off an operation like this. He was too lazy and impulsive to have the patience for anything that required planning. But he definitely hated and resented her. And one of her kidnappers *had* constantly smelled of alcohol, sometimes beer, sometimes liquor.

What disturbed her the most was his mention of a silent partner. Who would invest in Ralph's store? It didn't take a genius to see it was sinking like a stone. As long as Ralph was in charge, no amount of money would help.

Which meant that the 'investment' had likely been in payment for something else. Like a hand in her abduction? But who could the partner be? Laura? If Laura had been acting out of revenge for her firing, surely she would have needed more time to plan something as complex as an abduction. Not to mention that she was knocked unconscious at the same time that Robyn had been grabbed. No, Laura seemed an unlikely partner.

It was a few minutes before eight when Robyn pulled up in front of Kleiner's Electric. It looked more desolate than ever. A 'Closed' sign hung crookedly on the inside of the door, and one of the lights illuminating the window display had gone out which struck Robyn as funny since it was an electrical supply store.

Next door, at Lacey's Linens, a woman of about sixty with tight gray/brown curls was locking up for the day. She placed her keys in her pocket and started to walk away.

Robyn got out of her car. "Excuse me. Do you know if Ralph Kleiner is in?"

The woman frowned, but stopped to answer. "The store's been closed all day."

"Closed? Isn't it usually open Monday?"

"Supposed to be. The young man who works here days has been by several times trying to get in. He came into my store and phoned, but still couldn't rouse Ralph. I even went out in the alley and checked his back door. It's locked up tight."

Robyn paused. Unfortunately, this sounded far too much like Ralph. "D'you have any idea where Ralph might have gone?"

The woman's face puckered up as if she'd swallowed a bug. "Mr. Kleiner and I weren't really on speaking terms . . . but it wouldn't be the first time he hasn't opened the store lately." She sniffed. "He's probably in the back . . . sleeping."

Robyn grimaced. What the woman meant was that Ralph was sleeping off a bender. Again.

"Thank you." The woman turned and walked away.

Robyn got into her car, and drove around back to the narrow service alley. Lights shone over several back doors, but the alley was empty except for a couple of dumpsters and bundles of flattened boxes. The light was out over

Ralph's rear door, but two small casement windows high overhead in the back of the storeroom wall were open. It was still too light outside to tell if the lights were on inside.

She stopped the car and got out. As the neighboring storeowner had said, the steel door was locked, but she pounded on it anyway. "Ralph! Can you hear me, Ralph? Open up. It's Robyn."

There was no response. When she put her ear to the door, she could hear nothing from inside. She called the store number on her cell. It rang six times before voice mail clicked in and an annoying female voice said the mailbox was full.

She cut off the call and banged on the door. For good measure, she kicked it a few times, but still nothing. Ralph had to be inside. His car, an ancient station wagon with fake wood paneling, was parked a few spaces down from the store. God forbid, Ralph never walked anywhere.

The open windows near the top of the high ceiling of the stock room attracted her attention once more. Like it or not, she was worried. Even if Ralph had drunk steadily all weekend and passed out, he should be awake by now. Unless he'd fallen and hurt himself. Or worse, drunk himself to death.

She got back into her Beetle and parked it as close to the back wall of the building as she could. After crawling out the passenger door, she climbed onto the hood, and then onto the roof. Even standing on tiptoe, only her nose reached the sill. She slid down the side of the car, and climbed back up a moment later with a heavy plastic box of tools and emergency supplies that George had insisted she keep in her trunk. Standing on the box would give her the height she needed to see inside.

Finally, on tiptoe, and her fingers grasping the sill, she was able to look down into the room below. The lamp on Ralph's desk provided the only light. Wherever he was, it wasn't sitting at his desk. The executive style office chair Ralph favored had been pushed to one side of the desk. There was –

Robyn squinted downwards. What was that, between the desk and the chair? From this angle and with the room's shadows, it was difficult to tell. Was that a . . . a leg?

She clutched the windowsill. "Ralph," she shouted. "Ralph? Can you hear me?"

The leg didn't move. Nor was there any sound.

The strong odor of beer wafted upwards. Beer and something else she didn't like.

Vomit.

Shaking, she dropped from the window and slid off the car. She pulled out her cell and called 911.

The dispatcher came on the line.

"I need help," Robyn gasped. "There's a dead or sick man locked in the back of Kleiner's Electric Store!"

CHAPTER EIGHTEEN

A few minutes after one a.m. Will walked from the garage into the dimly lit house. Before he could shut the door, Robyn launched herself at him, burrowing into his arms and knocking him back against the wall. Her mouth sought his before he could say a word, and hungrily he returned her kisses. It was only when he gripped her bare arms that he realized she was cold and shaking.

He rubbed his hands up and down her arms. "You're cold," he said. "Come on. Let's get you covered up."

She shivered. "I haven't been able to get warm since .."

"Yeah, I know." He kissed her again and steered her into the living room. The cashmere blanket that had been a wedding present from Aunt Marcy lay on the sofa where she'd dropped it. He picked it up, wrapped it around her shoulders, then sat down and pulled her into his lap. "Better now?"

"Mmm, much." Her reply was lost in another kiss. When this one ended, she tilted her head against his cheek. "Thanks for coming. I didn't want to be alone tonight."

Will nuzzled her cheek. Her request meant so much to him. Because she had called him, not someone else. Because she had trusted him to come to her aid. Despite the charges against him. Despite Vince's death. Despite everything.

"Tell me all about it," he said."

She did. The flow of words started slowly, haltingly, then increased to a torrent. The firemen breaking down the door. The paramedics finding Ralph dead and wedged between his desk and the chair, the floor around him littered with empty cans of Miller, and a bottle of vodka. The stench of vomit and excrement."

"I still can't believe it. Robyn looked out the window into the dark night. "Not that Ralph is dead, but that he died like this. One of the firemen told me it looked like alcohol poisoning. But it wasn't unusual for Ralph to finish off two or three cases of beer over a weekend. I always thought he'd die an alcoholic, but not this soon. Not like this."

She swallowed. "The police mentioned something about an autopsy, so I guess we'll find out exactly how he died."

She paused again. "You know, I never really thought Ralph could have masterminded my abduction, but I can't stop this gut feeling he was a participant. Especially after that crack he made about having a secret partner. At least one of the people holding me on that island had alcohol on his breath all the time. Not only that, but I remember the floor shaking when one of them was walking around. Only a heavy person could do that. Ralph easily weighed more than three hundred pounds."

Her breath came out in a whoosh. "But I still can't see him killing Vince. He might kill someone in a drunken rage, but it would be with his fists, not a gun or knife. So who does that leave us with as suspects?"

Will stopped stroking her hair. "There's still Sergei."

Robyn shook free and gave him a pointed look. "Okay, let's stop pussy footing around my father. What about Raul? What have you found out about him?"

Will raised his hands. "I admit it. I am suspicious of your father. But I've looked into his background, and so far, nothing. It's Sergei who raises flags. Even then, the question is still why? He doesn't need the money. By all accounts he's a millionaire. And there's nothing to indicate he might have murdered Vince."

Robyn tilted her head and regarded Will as if she were assessing his likely reaction. "This seems almost too ridiculous to mention," she said. "But Sergei did ask me to marry him."

"What?" Will sat upright as his spine stiffened. "When did this happen?"

"It was shortly after we met. He was drunk at the time. You know, all that straight vodka he drinks."

"Why didn't you tell me?" he demanded.

Robyn's eyes met his without wavering. "Probably for the same reason you didn't tell me that my father tried to buy you off. Because I didn't want to upset you."

Will paused. Robyn was right. Both of them had tried to protect each other from hurtful news. Tried too hard, it seemed in retrospect. But that didn't stop him from wanting to warn Sergei off in no uncertain terms.

She continued. "Sergei has never mentioned it since. And really, it makes no sense as a reason to kidnap me. Why would –"

"Why indeed?" muttered Will. The court order had already made him a husband in name only. Now he learned another man – a man who could be around Robyn any time he chose – had tried to steal her from him only months before their wedding. Probably was <u>still</u> trying to win her over. It was bad enough her father was trying to convince her to divorce him every chance he got.

He looked hard at Robyn. "Just stay away from him, all right?"

Robyn didn't flinch. "Listen to me, Will," she said quietly. "It's you I want, not him. And always will be."

Will wanted to believe her, but he didn't trust his ability to talk calmly about Sergei right now. He shifted her off his lap. "I'd better get going. Dad may need the car first thing."

"Not yet." Robyn crawled back into his lap and twined her arms around his neck. She rested her forehead against his, her rich brown eyes beseeching. "Please, not yet."

Slowly, coaxed by the love in her eyes and the warmth of her body so close to his, Will relinquished his anger. How could he resist the woman he loved?

≈≈≈

The far off chime of a doorbell pierced the cocoon of warm contentment surrounding Robyn. The chimes went on and on, growing louder by the second, but Robyn ignored them and snuggled deeper into Will's embrace.

Suddenly Will catapulted upright. "Get up, Robyn. Someone's at the door. I've got to get out of here."

Fully awake now, Robyn sat up. She'd known it was dangerous to stay entwined in each other's arms after they'd made love, but she hadn't wanted to resist. Somehow the intended few minutes had stretched into hours and they'd fallen asleep. She glanced at the clock in the lightening room. 7:05!

She vaulted out of bed and grabbed her short kimono. On the other side of the bed, Will was pulling on his jeans. She threw on the robe and knotted the tie at her waist. "You stay here. I'll get rid of whoever's at the door."

She hurried to the front door. A glance through the peephole revealed the last person she wanted to see: Sergei!

Plastering a calm look on her face, she swung open the door. Sergei, looking trim in a short-sleeved shirt, striped tie, and dark dress trousers, smiled the moment he saw her. Behind him in the drive sat a dark-colored BMW, its motor running.

"I thought you and Raul were still in Argentina," she said curtly.

"I came back yesterday." His curious gaze traveled over her and she struggled to keep from squirming. Surely nothing indicated she'd just made love to Will?

"Raul won't be here for a couple more days," he continued. "After I heard the news, I had to find out if you were okay."

"What news? Oh. You mean Ralph's death?"

"It was on the radio this morning, while I was getting dressed. The announcer said Ralph had been found dead in the back of his store – and that you discovered the body."

He subjected her to another visual examination, as if he were looking for an injury. His gaze lingered on her bare legs exposed by the thigh-length robe. "Are you all right?"

"I'm fine now," she said. "It was quite a shock finding him like that, but I guess I should have known."

"Should have known what?" His eyebrows arched in puzzlement as he raised a hand to push back a lock of his hair. Two of his knuckles were discolored.

"That he'd drink himself to death. I just never expected it to happen so soon."

She straightened. "Thanks for coming out here. But I've really got to get going. I'm late already."

The corners of his mouth turned up "No time for a coffee?"

She shook her head. "Sorry. I was just getting dressed when you rang the doorbell. I'll be leaving in five minutes." To forestall argument, she issued an invitation. "How about coming by the club at eleven? We could go for coffee then."

"It's a date." His smile widened and he turned and headed for his BMW. Robyn shut the door, but stood listening beside it until she heard the car drive away.

She ran for the bedroom and shut the door.

"Who was that?" Will looked up from tying his running shoes.

"Sergei. He's gone now. He just left."

Will grimaced. "Did he give any indication he knew I was here? You know he'd report me to the police in a minute."

Robyn grabbed some pale yellow yoga pants from a drawer, and a matching yellow tee and jacket. "If he knew you were here, he wasn't letting on. He said he came out because he heard on the radio about Ralph."

"Hmm." Will paused. "It's probably best if I leave Dad's car here in the garage for now. I'll go into town with you, in the back seat under a blanket. If Sergei's waiting somewhere along the way, he won't see me."

Three minutes later Robyn had dressed, brushed her teeth, tamed her hair with water and conditioner and pulled it back into a ponytail. In the garage, just before they got into her car, Will pulled her to him for a ravenous kiss. Reluctantly, she disentangled herself from his arms and unlocked the car.

"Lie down and cover yourself up."

Will sighed. "Ah, the words every man wants to hear from his wife." He got down on the seat and covered himself with the gray blanket.

A moment later Robyn pulled out of the garage. Gravel crunched under the wheels, and then she was on the road, picking up speed.

"Was Sergei driving that blue BMW?" a muffled voice asked from the back.

"Yes."

"Keep your eyes open for it. If you think Sergei's following us, don't let me off at Dad's house. There's an empty shed a couple of blocks over where I can get out without being seen."

Robyn saw at least two cars that could have been Sergei's in the distance behind her. The first one turned onto another street after a couple of blocks. When the second one pulled up behind her, she could see the driver was a woman. But she was sufficiently rattled to not take any chances.

When they reached John Ryder's neighborhood, she followed Will's directions and backed into the shed that looked as if a strong wind would blow it flat as easily as a dead palm tree. Will threw back the blanket and got out.

Before she could say anything, he leaned in through the window and captured her lips in another of those soul-wrenching kisses that left her weak and wanting more.

He kissed her nose, his eyes gleaming, and stood up. "See you soon."

Then he was gone, out the back door of the shed.

Robyn hung onto the steering wheel and sighed. Soon couldn't come fast enough.

≈≈≈

Late afternoon the next day, Robyn put down the phone in her office and sighed. Forced separation from Will was doing weird things to her. Now just the sound of his voice over the phone was making her melt like butter on a Fort Zachary rock in the hot sun.

She sighed again. The information he'd communicated certainly hadn't been responsible for turning her into a puddle. At her request, Will had visited his eldest aunt, Clara Yundt. She was in a private room at the Key West Health and Rehabilitation on Stock Island, a frail old lady every bit as confused as Izzie had said. He sat and talked to her for close to an hour, trying every subject from the weather to the sale of her house to the nursing home's social schedule.

For the most part she was non-responsive, the eyes in the pale face clouded and half-closed. Only the mention of the shark processing camp on Wisteria elicited even a flicker of interest, but it had lasted only seconds before she'd fallen back into listlessness. It didn't surprise Robyn that Will had left not only disappointed, but dismayed at the old woman's condition. Robyn drummed her fingers on the desk. She and Will were fast running out of suspects. She had yet to pursue Laura but the truth was, she really couldn't see her as either a kidnapper or a killer. Sergei, annoying as he was, remained at best a maybe. And no matter how much Raul urged her to divorce Will, she just couldn't see her father as the kidnapper either, much less a killer. Why would he have paid her ransom as well as paid for her wedding? No, it didn't make sense.

The only person she truly believed could be involved was Ralph, and now he was dead. And then there was Vince. He was dead too, and if it wasn't suicide, no one was saying. But that was an idea she couldn't wrap her head or her heart around, any more than she could accept that Will might use her to rip off her --

A rap at the office door interrupted her thoughts. "Come in," she said absently.

To her dismay, not a staff member or client but Special Agent Rolland and Jamieson, his counterpart from the Monroe County Sheriff's Office, sidled into her office. With his hunched shoulders and crumpled suit, Rolland looked even gloomier than usual.

"Oh." The one word escaped before she could stop it. Her face and chest grew hot. Did they know she'd been seeing Will? She glanced at the phone. That she'd just talked to him? She swallowed. "What can I do for you gentlemen today?"

The two men stood just inside the door of her office, but she didn't invite them to sit down. They'd arrested Will, for God's sake. More and more it seemed like cases she'd read about, where investigators decided on the guilty person then spent all their efforts trying to find supporting evidence, rather than searching for the true criminal. In this case, who had *really* kidnapped her? Who had murdered Vince? And now Ralph?

"We'd like to ask you a few questions about Ralph Kleiner," Agent Rolland said. He nodded at the office chairs pushed up against Izzie's desk. "May we?"

She shrugged. "Go ahead."

The two men lowered themselves into the chairs, Jamieson's seat squealing in protest as it took his full weight. Once settled, Rolland took over again. "Mr. Kleiner is your ex-husband, right?"

"I told the Key West police that last night."

"How long have you been divorced?"

"Nine years. We were only together for two months."

"I understand he assaulted you. Badly."

Robyn's face flamed. She touched the scar on her left cheek. It wasn't something she liked to remember. "Yes."

"And yet you've kept in touch with him?"

"Not really. Until a few months ago, I hadn't talked to him for years."

"And what caused you to resume your relationship?"

Robyn's eyes narrowed. "We didn't 'resume' anything. Ralph saw the news stories about the success of Island Fit. His electrical store was failing. He started calling to ask for money. Finally I gave him six thousand dollars, hoping he'd go away."

"And did it work? Did Mr. Kleiner go away?"

"For about a month. Then the phone calls started again."

"Did you give him any more money?"

"No. Will paid him a visit and told him to leave me alone."

"Or what?"

Robyn gripped the arms of the chair. What was Rolland getting at? "I don't know. I guess that he'd call the police."

"So Will Ryder threatened Ralph, is that it?"

"No, that's not it at all." Robyn snapped upright like a rubber band. "Isn't that what the police are supposed to do? Protect people from harassment?"

Like a steamroller, Rolland continued. "Did your husband and Mr. Kleiner have a physical altercation?"

"No! " Robyn leapt to her feet. "Your questions are out of line, detective. And I'm done answering, at least until I have a lawyer present."

Rolland stood up too, and Jamieson lumbered to his feet beside him. From his six foot three inch height, Rolland looked down on her with annoying calmness.

"Fine, Ms. Locke, but we thought you'd be interested in knowing the circumstances of your ex-husband's death."

"What circumstances? He drank himself to death."

Rolland nodded solemnly. "No doubt Mr. Kleiner was a heavy drinker. But from the results of the autopsy, it doesn't look as if it's the alcohol that killed him. At least not the kind that you drink."

"What?"

"Mr. Kleiner was poisoned by isopropyl alcohol."

"Isopropyl alcohol?"

Rolland's small eyes zeroed in on hers.

"Rubbing alcohol, ma'am. Someone doctored his bottle of vodka with rubbing alcohol."

CHAPTER NINETEEN

"That's not good news no matter how you look at it." Will nodded glumly at his younger brother's assessment. Minutes after Special Agent Rolland had left Island Fit, Robyn had called Mark. The news that Ralph Kleiner had been poisoned – and that police considered Will a potential suspect – had them both rattled.

Mark grasped the sheet covering his broken legs. "After Vince's death, I thought they might be reconsidering the charges against you. Especially since my sources in the sheriff's office say they're not comfortable with the suicide theory. The written confession is just too pat."

He shook his head. "Aside from Vince's secret visits to the casino – and there were only a few - Federenko's P.I. hasn't found any evidence of outstanding loans, skimming or borrowing from your company or even from criminal elements. Even with your business's lost contracts, there's nothing to suggest that Vince was driven to kidnapping for financial reasons. Or you, for that matter."

He frowned. "But now I'm starting to think the police are developing tunnel vision. They've got you in their sights and they're obsessed with pinning whatever they can on you."

Will straightened. "Well, it's not going to work. The kidnapping charges are bad enough, but no one's getting away with Vince's murder. Now that Kleiner has been killed too, I can't help thinking he's tied in not only to the kidnapping, but also to Vince's murder. He knew something, and someone's killed him to shut him up."

His gaze met Mark's. After a long pause, Mark spoke softly. "You're thinking Robyn's father, right?"

Will nodded; Mark sighed. "The idea has appeal, but you know there's nothing to back it up."

"Raul hates my guts." Will straddled the armless office chair, resting his arms on the back as he rolled towards Mark glaring into the wall behind him.

"So what? Fathers hate their prospective son-in-laws all the time, but they don't kidnap and kill to keep their daughters from marrying – at least not in this country."

"What about Raul's proposal to invest in Robyn's fitness club and turn it into a nationwide chain?" Will persisted. "He was pissed off when she wanted to wait a year or two."

"Again, as a reason, it doesn't wash." Mark's voice started to fade. "Why would anyone abduct or kill because an investment was refused? There are lots of other places he could invest. Besides, Robyn did accept his offer, just not right now."

Mark sank back down against the pillows. His eyes shut. Will winced. He hadn't meant to wear Mark out with his frustrated ranting. His brother had enough to do just to contend with the pain and immobility and getting well.

Will got up to pull the sheet up over his brother's torso. His eyes still shut, Mark continued in a whispering voice. "And then there's Sergei. No doubt, as a former cop and now a security consultant, he has the skill to carry out a kidnapping or murder. But again, unless he's a homicidal maniac, the question is why? What does he get out of it?"

"Thanks for listening, Mark." Will patted his brother's arm. "You need to rest now."

The only answer was the regular rise and fall of his brother's chest.

Will turned back to the desk. Time to get on the computer and find the proof that had to be out there, somewhere.

≈≈≈

Leading the next morning's Advanced Yoga Practice, Robyn worked up twice the sweat she normally did. Maybe it had something to do with the ninety degree humid heat outside that strained the air conditioners. Maybe it was a result of her lousy sleep last night. Missing Will. Worrying about the new police suspicions. She wiped her brow with a towel as she headed to the private shower and washroom off her office.

She was halfway to the door when Candice hailed her from the reception desk. "Your father's on the phone from Argentina. I'm transferring the call to your office now."

Robyn hung the towel around her neck and entered the office. On cue, the phone rang. What did Raul want now?

Reluctantly she picked up the receiver. "Hi, Raul. How are you?"

"Robyn. Robyn? Is that you?"

She held the phone away from her ear. The connection was poor, but Raul's shouting only made the crackles and hisses sound worse.

"Yes, I can hear you," she enunciated slowly. "You don't need to shout."

"Listen," he yelled. "I will arrive in Key West in two days. Until then I want you to go to the Marquesa Hotel. I've already asked Sergei to book a room for you beside his."

She rolled her eyes. Sergei had to have phoned him with the news that Ralph had been murdered. "That isn't necessary."

Even across the phone line, Robyn could hear Raul's incredulity. "But Sergei says that Kleiner man – your ex-husband – has been murdered. That's the second death of someone close to you in the last two weeks. You cannot stay alone."

"I'll be fine," Robyn said patiently. "You know how good my new security system is."

"That's not enough. Not with your . . . with Will Ryder on the loose. What if you are abducted again? Or worse, murdered?"

"That's ridiculous."

"Please. Please go to the Marquesa." Her father's voice broke. "Let Sergei take care of you. He knows how important you are to me. He'll guard you with his life."

Robyn rolled her eyes again. For years she'd desperately wanted a father. Now she had one, he was driving her crazy."

She took a deep breath. "Raul, I'm staying in my own home. I'll be fine. Truly. I'm not a little girl. You have to stop worrying about me, okay?"

"No, it is not okay. It's –"

The crackling and hissing rose to a crescendo drowning out his words. After a minute of listening to ear-grating static, Robyn hung up.

She headed for the shower. For once, she hoped her father wouldn't call back.

≈≈≈

Will arrived at Mark's place mid-afternoon the next day, after finishing a job replacing rotten floorboards on a porch. He enjoyed doing repairs as much as restoration work, but without Vince it wasn't the same. He missed his support, his hard work and attention to detail, his dry sense of humor. It was hard to set his sorrow aside and get on with the job when every tool he picked up, every nail and screw, made him think of Vince.

Mark was dozing when Will bid the home care worker goodbye and settled in at his younger brother's computer. He wouldn't wake him; Mark put on a good show, but he was in pain, his legs still swollen, and he tired easily. His secretary came every morning for a couple of hours, but even the small amount of work they got through wore him out.

Will brought up the browser and stared blindly at the home page. Last night he had gone to every reference to Raul Leopoldo and Sergei Kakovka he could find. He'd finally given up on Sergei – the little there was in English he'd already read and the rest was in Russian and inaccessible to him without a translator – and concentrated on Raul. But he'd already hit every promising reference and had come up empty.

So what to do? Give up and pursue another suspect? But he couldn't shake the idea that somehow, some way, Raul Leopoldo was behind everything that had happened. Including the murders of Vince and Ralph. Robyn didn't believe it, but no matter how much he loved her, he couldn't afford to spare her feelings any longer.

No, the only thing to do was review every site he'd visited, searching for that one elusive fact that he hoped he had overlooked and the key that would help him find the truth.

He started back at square one, visiting the website of Leopoldo and De Guzman, Inc. He reread every word, clicked on every link, to no avail. He was about to declare defeat and review some of the online articles in English about Raul when he noticed a link near the bottom of the home page. LDG World Wide Services, it read in very small nondescript type. There was nothing else, and the link wasn't listed under any of the home page tabs. He remembered seeing the name in his last search, but for some reason hadn't followed it.

This time he did, the company name unfurling across a discreet gray background. Beneath it scrolled the words "Security Services Around the World". Clicking on the company name brought Will to another page, this one providing a brief listing of services: installation and maintenance of security and surveillance systems; training in security procedures; provision of security forces; and personal security equipment. He clicked on the 'Contact Us' link, and brought up listings in four countries: Argentina, Brazil, Chechnya, and the United States.

The Buenos Aires address didn't surprise Will. It was the same address as the head office for Leopoldo and De Guzman, Inc. But the Florida address was a surprise.

It was in Marathon, an hour or so drive up the keys from Key West. To Will's knowledge, neither Robyn nor her father had ever mentioned Raul going to Marathon for business.

Will studied the address for a long time. Why did it sound so familiar? He'd been in and out of Marathon all his life, but he knew that wasn't why he recognized the name.

Out of the blue, it came to him. He got up and rifled through a stack of local newspapers. In the section highlighting contractors in the Key West Citizen, he found the large ad for Cardinal Security. His eyes widened when he saw the address: It was the same as the one listed on the World Wide Services website.

World Wide Services *was* Cardinal Security. And Cardinal Security had installed a security system in his home just days before the wedding as part of the wrap up of the home's restoration.

The security system that someone could circumvent to access his computer and printer to write those ransom notes!

≈≈≈

At ten after seven in the evening, Robyn pulled into her driveway and halted abruptly. Sergei Kakovka, his broad face split by a welcoming grin, sat on a bench by the front door on the porch that wrapped around three sides of the house.

Robyn cussed. Of all the people she didn't want to see right now, he was at the top of the list. She left the engine running and hopped out. "What are you doing here?" she demanded.

Sergei's smile evaporated. He dropped the arms spread across the back of the bench to his sides. "That's not much of a welcome," he responded.

"It's not a welcome at all. I know Raul sent you, and I don't want or need you here. Go away."

Sergei's face drooped and he raised his hands in exasperation. "Now I am hurt. Out of concern for you, I have been waiting here for more than an hour. I promised your father I would stay here all night. And you tell me to go away?"

As his hands dropped back to his lap, a glint of something dark at his waist caught Robyn's attention. Her throat seized up. "That . . . that's . . . you've got a gun!"

"Actually it's a semi-automatic pistol. A Glock 17." His eyes turned the same dark gray of the weapon. "Two people have died and you've been kidnapped in the last few weeks. I told Raul I'd protect you."

"You . . . you can't stay here with that. Someone might get hurt." Her voice rose. *Will, for instance.* He was coming here at midnight.

Sergei took the Glock from the waistband of his jeans and nonchalantly looked through the sights. "That's the general idea."

He set it down on his thigh, and looked at her, his eyes narrowed. "Especially if Will Ryder shows up."

A chill ran down Robyn's spine. Nothing about Sergei's demeanor suggested he was anything but serious. She straightened. "I don't want you lurking around my door with a gun. If you're not gone in five minutes, I'm calling the police."

He tucked the gun back into his jeans and sat back. He smiled pleasantly. "No, you won't. Especially since I'll be telling them about your husband's illegal midnight visits."

A sick feeling settled in her stomach like a stone. "You're crazy," she sputtered. "Crazy and wrong!"

"Am I?" He tilted his head and studied her, his gray eyes cool and calculating. She wondered how she'd ever found him the least bit engaging.

His voice dropped to a purr. "I might be willing to take your word for it if you invited me in for dinner and a drink."

"No!" She stomped over to her car, and drove into the garage. Through the rearview mirror she watched to make sure he didn't slip inside while she closed the garage door.

As soon as she left the garage she unlocked the side door and disarmed the alarm. Inside, she reset the alarm and hurried into the kitchen. She dropped her purse on the island, grabbed the phone and pressed in Mark's number. After five rings, Sam answered.

"Is Will there?" Robyn demanded.

"No, he's not. Is something wrong?"

"No. No, it's okay." Robyn forced herself to slow down. "Can you ask Mark where he's gone?"

"Sure." Robyn heard a muffled exchange in the background then Sam came back on the line. "Will's drove up to Marathon this afternoon. Something about business."

"When will he be back?"

"He's not coming back, at least not here. I imagine he'll go straight to his Dad's."

"Thanks, Sam. Give my love to Mark."

Robyn hung up and stared at the phone. Should she try Will's cell? She hated to do it, especially from home, because then there'd be a record. But she couldn't risk Will coming here with Sergei waiting outside the front door with a gun. The close call with Will at the house the other morning had been scary enough.

She pressed in Will's number and waited impatiently while the phone rang once, twice, five times, before the computerized voice came on the line. "Your call has been forwarded to an automated voice message system . . ."

She hung up and looked at the clock. It was only seven-thirty; plenty of time to head Will off.

At nine o'clock, after picking at a salad, while watching one of her favorite movies, 'Rodeo Girl' starring Katherine Ross and flipping disinterestedly through the latest issues of *People* and *Self,* Robyn checked the driveway entrance from a window in the guest bedroom. Dammit! Sergei was still sitting there, like a statue with nowhere to go.

A surge of irritation propelled her to the door. After she disarmed the door, she flung it open and glared at him. "You know you're wasting your time!"

He yawned and raised his arms in a stretch that highlighted his muscular biceps. When he resettled himself, he smiled. "That's a matter of opinion." His voice lowered seductively. "Now if you asked me in, we could both do something far more productive . . . and interesting . . . with our time."

His lascivious gaze traveled over her, leaving no doubt about his meaning. "No way." She recoiled, slammed the door, and collapsed against it, her head in her hands.

After a moment to recharge, she barreled into the kitchen to phone Mark again. Sam picked up immediately. "Will's not here and Mark is asleep. Can I give Will a message if he shows up?"

"Yes, please. Tell him . . . tell him Sergei's outside our house." She paused. "With a gun."

"What?" Sam's voice rose. "That doesn't sound good. Have you called the sheriff?"

Robyn didn't know how much Sam knew but didn't want to drag her into it. "Please, just give Will the message. It's important, all right?"

"Sure. Anything else?"

"No. I've got to go."

Robyn hung up and dialed John Ryder's home. The phone rang and rang. In desperation she tried Will's cell again. After several rings, the computerized voice clicked in again. "Your call has been —"

Robyn hung up. She glanced at the phone. Nine fifteen. Surely Sergei wouldn't sit outside for another three hours. Surely she'd be able to reach Will by then.

For the next two hours, Robyn tried John Ryder's number and Will's cell every ten minutes. With each unanswered call she grew more agitated, and more fearful for Will's safety. He couldn't come here, not with Sergei sitting outside.

At eleven twenty she checked outside through the guest bedroom window. In the light from the lantern light fixtures outside the front door, she could see Sergei clearly. He not only was awake and alert, he was whistling the chorus to some melancholic Russian sounding folk song.

The whistling grated on her nerves. She couldn't wait any longer. She had to do something – anything – to prevent Sergei from harming Will.

She took a deep breath and went straight to the liquor cabinet in the brightly painted sideboard in the dining room. She took out a full bottle of Gray Goose vodka, a shot glass, and an old-fashioned glass. Stopping in the kitchen, she dumped ice into her glass, and a splash of orange juice then headed for the front door.

She glanced in the mirror, and blinked at the grim look on her face. Carefully she schooled her features into a calm, pleasant expression. Maybe she couldn't force Sergei to leave. Maybe she couldn't warn Will away. But there was one thing she could do.

She swung the door open and lifted the bottle in Sergei's direction. On her face was a smile that felt as artificial as a plastic mask.

"Since you won't leave, how about a night cap? I hate to drink alone."

Sergei cut the whistling mid note. "So you finally decided to take pity on me? You're a hard woman, Robyn Locke."

She filled the shot glass to the brim with vodka, and handed it to him. He threw it back in one gulp then held out the glass for more, his eyes shining. Silently she refilled it then splashed a small amount of vodka into her own glass already three-quarters full with ice and orange juice. The plan was to get Sergei drunk, or at least distract him, so Will would have a fighting chance of escaping unseen.

He threw the second glass down with lightening speed then patted the bench beside him. Robyn sat down gingerly. Mata Hari she wasn't, but she'd do whatever necessary to keep Will safe.

Sergei took the bottle out of her hands and filled his shot glass again. This time he raised it in a toast and clinked his glass against Robyn's. His gleaming gray eyes met hers. "To beautiful American women. To you."

"To me." She raised her glass and sipped a small amount. She glanced at her watch. Only eleven forty-one. How long before he started feeling the effects of the alcohol? Surely if he kept drinking at this pace, it wouldn't be long.

Sergei downed this shot and poured another. Raising her eyebrows in what she hoped was an innocent expression, she asked, "Don't you think you should slow down?"

"Ha!" He laughed and gulped another shot. He gestured expansively. "To a true Russian, vodka is like water. The water of life. Vodka makes a man stronger, braver, more daring."

He poured another shot and downed it too, then smiled at her with a lewdness that turned her stomach. "And of course, you know that vodka makes a man more virile."

Without warning, he took her drink, set the two glasses on the floor then raised her hand to his lips. His gaze on her, he brushed his wet lips across her knuckles. "Why do you keep resisting? You know I am wild for you, Robyn. And I am a real man – a Russian man – not like that nothing Will Ryder."

She tried to object, but he moved swiftly, covering her mouth with a wet, sloppy kiss. She heard breaking glass and forced herself to ignore her natural inclination to shove him off. One of his big hands tangled in her hair, while the other grasped for her breast through her thin t-shirt.

He thrust his tongue down her throat and it was all she could do not to gag. Her hands slipped around his back. In a pretense of massaging his back, she lowered her hands to his waist. Her left wrist hit the grip of the pistol. Without hesitation she grasped it.

But before she could pull it out of his waistband, a hand like a steel vise clamped around her.

"And what is this?" his moist, vodka-laced voice whispered against her ear. "You're –"

Without warning Sergei's words broke off. His big body jerked back from hers. His grip loosened on her wrist and she yanked the gun free.

"Get the hell away from my wife." A fist flashed by her and crashed into the side of Sergei's head.

CHAPTER TWENTY

The moment Will saw Robyn and Sergei drinking on the bench outside the front door, he suspected what Robyn was doing. Thank God he'd parked the panel truck at the car rental place down the street and walked the rest of the way.

He was about to circle around to the back of the house and let himself in when Sergei raised Robyn's hand to his lips. Will froze.

When the Russian pulled Robyn into his arms and kissed her, Will's self-control exploded. He pelted across the drive, grabbed Sergei by the shoulders and yanked him off Robyn.

Sergei teetered on the edge of the bench. Before he could regain his balance, Will punched him in the side of the head.

Sergei fell to the ground. With the reflexes of a fit and trained fighter, he rolled to his knees and sprang to his feet. His right hand flew to the belt of his jeans.

"Don't bother looking for your gun." Robyn's voice, calm and steady, came from behind the Russian. "I've got it."

Will looked at Robyn. In her hand was the semi-automatic pistol, her finger on the trigger. It was pointed at Sergei.

Sergei took a step towards Robyn.

"Don't move or I'll shoot!"

Robyn's fierce calm amazed Will, though he detected the slightest of tremors in her voice.

The Russian glared at Will. "Enjoy your last moments of freedom, Ryder. The police will hear of this assault – and that you've broken the conditions of your bail."

Will snorted. "Do your worst Sergi. While you're at it, maybe you can explain to the sheriff why you're carrying a semi-automatic pistol outside my wife's door."

Sergei looked at Robyn. "Give me back my pistol."

"Get the hell out of here," Will cut in. "Or I'll be the one calling the police. It'll be worth going to jail just to see you arrested.

Sergei cast another pleading glance Robyn's way, but she ignored him. "You heard Will." She gestured to the road with the pistol. "Beat it."

His expression livid, Sergei stalked to the road. A moment later the roar of a car engine sounded from Southernmost Point. A dark BMW shot past the entrance to the drive, heading in the direction of Duval.

"You'd better go too, Will. He's going to call the police. I know it." Robyn lowered the gun.

Will grimaced. "Yeah. I know." He walked to Robyn's side and reached up and stroked her silken cheek pausing at the scar he so loved. "I hate to leave you here alone."

"I doubt I'll be alone for long."

Her brown eyes burned with concern for him. "But what about you? Where will you go? Once Sergei reports you, the police will be looking for you."

"Not my Dad's or Mark's, that's for sure." He smiled as reassuringly as he could. "I'll figure out something. Don't worry."

He brushed her lips with his own. For a brief moment, he held her tightly.

"What if Sergei comes back?" he asked as he released her.

"He won't."

Robyn grinned at him and raised the pistol. "I've got his gun."

≈≈≈

"Hello?"

Will sagged with relief at the sound of Robyn's voice over the phone line. It was six thirty a.m. She sounded wary, but all right.

"Are you alone?"

"Yes. The sheriff's deputies never showed up last night. Not this morning either. What do you think that means?"

"I don't know," Will said unhappily. "I slept in my rental truck in Key Haven."

"It's got to be the gun," theorized Robyn. "Sergei can't have a permit for it and he certainly can't just wander around with it. He wants to immigrate here. Maybe he's afraid the gun will ruin his chances."

The reminder of the Glock made Will even more uneasy. "What are you going to do with it?"

"I was hoping the sheriff would take it away, but since they haven't come . . ." She paused. "Maybe I'll bury it."

Will wasn't happy with a loaded gun anywhere near Robyn. But they didn't have a safe, or any place they could lock it up. "Just be sure to remove the magazine and bury it somewhere else. And make sure no one sees you."

He halted. "Did Sergei come back?"

245

"No."

"Good."

Will paused again. Should he tell Robyn what he'd found out on his trip to Marathon last night? That a division of her father's company had bought out the business that installed their new security system. And that the former owner of the company, who'd been kept on to run it, had been given a big check to just walk away three days before their system was installed.

"What about tonight, Robyn?" he asked, while he considered what to tell her. "I'd be a lot happier if you stayed downtown with Izzie."

"Raul will be back tonight," she said. "I know he'll come straight to the house. I'll be fine."

Raul again. Will mulled that over. He couldn't object without telling her about Cardinal Security. But was that enough to warn her away from her father? Would she see it as anything more than a coincidence? The division that had bought Cardinal Security wasn't even run by her father, but by his partner De Guzman.

"Okay," he said finally, "but call me if you have any problems. Any at all."

"But your cell –"

"I'm so sorry. With all this upheaval, I have misplaced my charger. I have to get back to Dad's or Mark's today to find it. If I can't, I'll pick up a new one this afternoon I promise. And I'll get Mark's secretary to find out if there's a warrant out for my arrest."

After a few more words, Will replaced the receiver in the cradle of the last remaining public phones on the island. He looked at the bruised and swollen knuckles of his right hand. For Robyn's sake, he hoped he'd made the right decision not to tell her about Raul and Cardinal Security.

≈≈≈

Robyn was waiting up for her father to call her upon his return to Key West around midnight when the phone rang.

It was Izzie.

"Robyn, thank God! You've got to come to the club right away."

"What's wrong?"

Everything had been fine when Robyn left after closing at nine. It was Izzie's first day back since her fall, and she'd stayed after hours to work out. Always embarrassed by her big bust and full hips, she preferred to exercise alone.

The answer was something between a gasp and a snort. "I'm stuck in one of the machines and I can't get out. I'm lucky my cell was in my pocket."

"Oh, Izzie." Robyn thought fast. "Why don't you call Candice? She lives only a few minutes away.

"It's embarrassing, all right? Just come, will you?" Izzie's exasperation shrilled over the line.

"All right. I'll be there in fifteen. Will you be okay for that long? I could call the fire department."

"No!" Izzie squealed. "D'you want me to die of embarrassment? Besides, the doors are locked."

"Okay, okay. I'll be there as fast as I can."

Robyn grabbed her bag from the kitchen and ran for the garage. A moment later she was on the road, headed downtown. It was only a few minutes after ten. She should be back in plenty of time to prepare herself for Raul's call

– something she anticipated with both dread and determination.

Because tonight she was telling him to lay off Will. No ifs, ands, or buts. Will was her husband, she loved him, and she refused to hear another word against him. He was no kidnapper, any more than Vince's death was a suicide. If Raul persisted in his accusations, then he would have to leave her alone. She loved him and would hate to lose the father she had waited to know for most of her life, but she had made her decision. She was standing by Will. She trusted him, and she trusted her own judgment.

As she drove downtown, she wondered where Will was tonight. He'd called her from a public phone this afternoon with the news there was no warrant out for his arrest. Sergei hadn't reported him, at least not yet. Was it because of the gun? She hoped so. The Glock was now buried as deep as she could get it into the coral rocks behind her house. She understood why locals affectionately call Key West 'living on the Rock'. The magazine was buried under a flaming red bougainvillea at the side of the house.

She turned into the club's lot and stopped the car right in front of the doors. She got out, sorted through her keys for the right one and reached for the door handle. To her surprise, it wasn't locked. Izzie must have been mistaken.

The lights had been turned off in the reception area, but full lighting blazed from the side of the building holding the resistance machines and weights. The treadmills and cross-trainers across from the offices cast long, weird shadows across the carpeted floor. As Robyn cut through them, she looked for Izzie in the lighted area. She didn't see her.

"Izzie?"

"Over here."

The strained croak came from the left, in the exercise area behind the open staircase. Robyn hurried around the staircase to the machinery and racks of kettlebells on the other side. Izzie lay in a leg press, her face red and sweating, her knees bent almost to her chest. On either side of the press held up by her feet were . . . more than three hundred pounds of weights.

"I . . . I can't . . . lift it off me," Izzie gasped. "You've . . . got . . . to help me."

Robyn stared at Izzie in horror. There was no point asking her how she'd gotten into this fix. The question was how to get her out. There was no way Robyn could lift the press high enough to slide in the safety bar and free Izzie. The only thing to do was remove the 45 pound weights, one at a time.

"Hang on, Iz." Robyn stuffed the keys in her pocket and reached for the weight closest to her.

"Not so fast."

Robyn whirled around. Her jaw dropped at the sight of the man who stood there, smiling. In his hand was a gun just like the one she'd buried in the rocks earlier today.

And it was pointed at her.

CHAPTER TWENTY-ONE

Try as he might, Will could find no direct link from LDG Worldwide Services and Cardinal Security to Raul Leopoldo. He'd gone as far as driving to Marathon this afternoon to show Jeff Newman, the former owner of Cardinal, photos of both Raul and Sergei. Jeff had never seen either man before. The person Jeff had done business with best met the description of Ralph Kleiner, though he'd gone by another name.

Now, his head aching and his eyes blurry, Will scrolled through yet another website in an effort to find that elusive link, the clue that would prove – or disprove – once and for all that Raul was the source of all his problems. But the more he read, the clearer it became that Raul had nothing to do with Worldwide Services, the security arm of Leopoldo and De Guzman, Inc. It had been Eduardo De Guzman's baby from the start, and nothing he found indicated anything else.

In desperation, Will started back where he'd begun, with the chatty online article, the only source of personal information in English he'd been able to find about the man. He read it over and over again. It was nine o'clock when he read it last, stopping at the reference to Raul's cattle ranch in Cordoba. The story called it his winter retreat. It's winter down in Argentina now, he thought dully. Why hasn't Raul been spending any time down there lately?

But he had been there, he remembered with a start. Or at least somewhere in Argentina. Robyn told him that Raul had gone back to Argentina recently. Funny, Raul had never spoken about the ranch in all the times he'd been around Will or Robyn. Nor had he shown any interest in the televised Texas rodeo contests a peculiar love of Robyn's this time of year.

Will went on to another website, but the image of the ranch and Raul as a rancher, refused to go away. Somehow, they just didn't fit. Any more than the letters Raul had written to Robyn's mother seemed to fit with the man he knew. Will believed in facts and figures, but he'd always trusted his gut reactions too. And his gut told him that there was something off about Raul the rancher, Raul the estranged but loving husband and father in letters.

Not quite sure why he was doing it, he conducted a search for ranches in Cordoba. Within five minutes, he had a phone number. He scrawled it on a piece of paper then questioned why he bothered. He couldn't call the number. He didn't speak Spanish.

A quiet laugh punctuated the murmur of conversation between Sam and Mark on the other side of the room. *But Sam did!* Sam's minor in college had been Spanish, and she kept her Spanish since there were so many opportunities to do so now in 'Cayo Hueso' the original name for Key West.

Will jumped up, crossed the room and thrust the scrap of paper in front of Sam's nose. "I need you to call this number in Argentina for me."

"Now?"

"Yes, now. It's the phone number for Raul Leopoldo's ranch in Cordoba. I want you to see if he's been there any time recently."

"Why?" Mark interrupted.

"Later. I'll explain later." Will turned to Sam. "If you get Raul, just say you're calling on behalf of his daughter Robyn Locke, who wants to know when he'll be back in the U.S. If you don't, ask whoever answers when he was there last. Okay?"

Sam placed the call and put it on speakerphone. She began speaking into the receiver, asking for Señor Raul Leopoldo in carefully enunciated Spanish.

She listened for a moment then began to repeat her question. Suddenly she stopped and frowned. "*Perdóne, puede hacer el favor de repetirlo?*"

From a few feet away, Will could hear the faint sound of an anguished, childish voice, and then what sounded like sobbing.

Abruptly the sobbing ended and a strident female voice came on, loud enough to be heard throughout the living room. "*Quién habla?*"

Grimacing, Sam gathered herself together to repeat the question that had elicited such a visceral reaction the first time. Will remembered enough Spanish from high school to know that she reintroduced herself and asked for Raul Leopoldo again.

Another response from the woman on the other end of the line made her wince. Slowly and carefully Sam asked another short question. Again Will and Mark could hear the woman speaking in Spanish. She sounded upset.

Sam tried again. She had spoken only a few words when she stopped speaking. She looked at the phone with indignation. "She hung up. The woman just hung up on me."

"What did she say?" demanded Will. "And what was that crying about?"

Quickly Sam filled them in on the little she'd gotten from the phone conversation.

It was enough to fuel Will's worst fears. Maybe it was true, maybe it wasn't, but Robyn needed to know.

And she needed to know *now*.

≈≈≈

To Robyn's surprise, Sergei laughed. "Why are you so shocked to see me?"

Her gaze darted from his oddly beaming face to the gun he held in his hand. It looked like the Glock she had buried in her yard this morning. "How . . . how did you get your gun back?"

He shook his head in amusement, as if he were dealing with a particularly slow child. "You think I have only one? Silly girl."

His tone confused her. She glanced nervously at Izzie, whose legs were folded up like an accordion. She was in serious pain. On impulse she decided to ignore the gun and accept Sergei's jarringly jovial demeanor at face value.

"Here, help me free Izzie." She turned to the leg press.

"Don't move."

Robyn glared at Sergei. "She's hurting. We've got to –"

"Not until I extract a promise from you."

"A promise?" She stared at him.

"Exactly." He nodded his head. "A promise that you will divorce Will and marry me."

"Are you insane?" The words burst out before Robyn could stop them.

Sergei's face flamed. With what looked like an effort, he assumed a tight-lipped smile. "Only if being in love with you is insane," he said curtly. As he spoke, he seemed to regain some of his confidence. His gray eyes locked with hers and his lips relaxed.

"Robyn, you know I've wanted you from the moment we met. We will make – how do you say – we will make beautiful music together, like a great symphony by Tchaikovsky."

Robyn blinked. "But . . . but that's imposs--"

"It's more than that, I agree. When it comes to you, I may be a romantic fool, but I am not just any fool. No, indeed." He straightened, and the lovesick look that had seized him for a moment disappeared. He looked bizarrely calm and menacing.

"No, marrying you is also good for business. With an American wife, my chances of getting a green card, as well as American citizenship, will improve immensely. It will be easier to bring in money from Russia, to invest, for example, in your club. And I will be able to supply more trained men and money for Raul's security operations around the world."

The mention of Raul jarred her, but she was still trying to wiggle out of Sergei's crazed marriage demand. Involuntarily she stepped away to put distance between them, but was stopped when her backside hit the York 5-80 kettlebell rack.

"Why me? Why not marry another American woman? Someone who's free? I'm sure –"

A low moan from Izzie cut her off. She turned to look. Izzie's battered face was beet red. Sweat dripped down her forehead, joining the tears dribbling from her eyes. Robyn reached for the closest weight.

"Stop!"

"But she's –"

"Don't move. I love you, but I have run out of patience." His left hand slid inside his light nylon jacket. He withdrew a sheaf of papers and a pen and held them out to Robyn. "Either you sign the application for divorce and agree to marry me, or both you and Izzie will die."

A terrified squeak came from behind Robyn. "He means it," gasped Izzie. "He's the one who beat me up last week. He killed –"

"Shut up!" Sergei's lip curled menacingly and his eyes oddly glittered. He jabbed the papers at Robyn. "Sign them now or die. If I can't have you, no one will have you."

Robyn took the papers and the pen. Without a word she found the spots marked with an "X" for her signature. Balancing the papers on her knee, she tried to sign her name. At first the pen wouldn't work. She shook it, and tried again, managing a shaky scrawl on each of the signature lines. Now was not the time to challenge Sergei. But she wished she could have picked up the phone ringing in the distance in her office. She instinctively knew it would not be a good idea to answer her vibrating cell in her pocket.

She straightened and handed the papers and pen to him. He glanced at the signatures then stuffed the papers back inside his jacket.

"Now will you help me get Izzie out?" she asked quietly.

"All right, my love. But no funny business or Izzie will be the first to go." His expression softened with his successful manipulation of Robyn.

"You take the weights off that side and I'll take them off this side."

As Sergei moved past her to the far side of the leg press, she reached behind her for a ten pound kettlebell. The second he turned his back she grabbed it and smashed it down on the back of his head, the impact jarring her arm all the way to the shoulder. He staggered but did not fall.

The next blow knocked him out and to the floor. The Glock skidded across the room and into the base of another machine.

Robyn hurried to Izzie. "Come on, we've got to get you out of here before your knees are totaled."

She grabbed the first weight. Her fingers had just closed around it when Izzie gasped. "Robyn –"

Robyn glanced down behind her. She saw a pair of shiny black shoes and the pressed cuffs of a man's navy suit. Her gaze lifted to the familiar face and her shoulders sagged with relief.

"Raul! Thank God you're here. Come and help me get these weights off Izzie."

A heavy sigh was the only answer. She turned back to freeing Izzie.

"Ah, *mi querida hija*. You make life so difficult."

Her fingers stopped working at Raul's odd words. Why wasn't he beside her, helping free his fiancé? She glanced back and blinked.

In his right hand, Raul held the gun that had flown out of Sergei's hand. Once again, it was pointed at her.

≈≈≈

Where was she?

Will had tried the phone at the house. He'd tried Robyn's cell. He'd called Island Fit. He'd done it all over again. No one answered anywhere.

In desperation, Will sped out to the house. He found it dark and empty and Robyn's car gone from the garage.

As he raced back to town, he tried all three numbers again. Still nothing. *Where could she be?*

Just before eleven p.m. he drove past Island Fit. Robyn's car was parked in front of the club doors, as if she'd pulled into the lot and run into the club without taking the time to park properly. Izzie's jeep was at the side of the lot, in a staff parking space.

Will parked on the street a half block away and ran back.

Across the street he noticed a dark BMW that looked a lot like the one Sergei drove.

He peered through the glass front doors. Lights blazed from the area housing the weight machines, part of which was hidden from his view by the open staircase to the second floor. The rest of the interior was in shadow. He couldn't see either Robyn or Izzie.

Quietly he tried the glass doors. They were unlocked. He slipped quietly through the right one then into the lobby, and stopped to listen. At first he heard nothing and then, as he strained harder, he thought the heard a man's voice, followed by a woman's. *Robyn?*

Silently he crossed the floor then hugged the wall of offices until he reached the stairs. Crouching, he climbed to the landing halfway up the stairs, hidden behind the waist-high wall. From there he could see into the spinning classroom and the weight machine area. He slid between the wall and the end of a narrow table displaying the ribbon-festooned stationary bicycle to be given as a prize in a membership recruitment contest.

Rising just enough to see over the wall, Will looked down at a strange tableau. Robyn stood beside a leg press, her attention frozen on something or someone near the wall beneath him. A woman was in the leg press, her legs pressed flat to her chest – Izzie, her face red and tear-streaked! On the floor on the other side of the leg press sprawled a man. He wasn't moving either, and it took a moment before Will realized it was Sergei.

Carefully he rose a little higher and looked down. Directly beneath him stood a man in a navy suit and white shirt, his dark hair shining in the overhead light. Raul! But why was no one moving? Why was –

The dark gray of the gun came into focus. Will froze. *That was why!*

He rose a little higher and strained to hear Raul's low voice, which had been droning on in what sounded like a lecture. What he heard was not reassuring.

"Like so many American women, you are too stubborn, too headstrong, for your own good. If only you had seen reason, we would not be standing here like this now."

Robyn's face was pale and stiff. Her voice sounded strained, but she made an effort at defiance. "What are you talking about?" she demanded. "What –"

"Let me out, Raul." A piteous mewling interrupted from the direction of the leg press. "My legs are going to break off."

Will glanced down at Izzie. Her face was redder than anything he'd ever seen, and oddly bruised and battered.

"That's right, *mi amor*," Raul continued smoothly. "Even your friend Izzie could see what was best for you. If only you had used your head from the start, none of this would have happened."

"Please get me . . ."

"Shut up, Izzie," Raul said without wasting a glance at her.

"What . . . what are you talking about?" Robyn looked bewildered. "If only I had used my head?"

"If you'd used your head and never married that bastard Will Ryder in the first place, none of this would have been necessary. Not the abduction, not the arrest of your husband . . . none of it."

A sigh punctuated Raul's statement. "And now you have put me in an untenable position. Unless you agree to divorce Will Ryder, marry Sergei, and let us immediately start investing in your business, I will have to take stronger measures to convince you."

Will could almost hear the smile in Raul's voice as he turned towards the leg press. "Starting with Izzie."

Robyn's eyes widened and her mouth gaped. "But . . . but she's your fiancé. She's –"

"Merely an expendable pawn in what's become an annoyingly complex operation. She's —"

"Believe him," sobbed Izzie. "He killed . . . he and Sergei killed Vince and Ralph! They tried to kill Mark!"

Robyn blanched. She looked as if she was going to throw up. Will clamped his lips shut to hold back the gasp of horror. He gripped the railing so hard his fingers turned white.

"You . . ." Robyn's agonized whisper hung in the air. "You . . . and Vince . . . and Ralph too?"

"Yes, and it's your fault," Raul replied briskly. "And Sergei's too, of course. If that Russian fool hadn't set his mind on marrying you and no one else, none of this would have been necessary. Sergei had the trained men and the money I needed to expand my security operations around the world. But once he met you and became so obsessed, he refused to deal unless you were part of the package."

Will's fury increased with every word Raul uttered. It pounded through his veins, echoing in his chest and in his head. His fingers itched to close around the throats of his brother's killers. Raul and that damned Russian had killed Vince and crippled Mark — for effing money — and now were threatening Robyn. His shoulder jabbed into the corner of the table displaying the stationary bike. He looked up at the bike, and then knew what he had to do.

"But . . . but I'm your daughter. You love me . . . my mother. How . . . how could you do this?"

The pain in Robyn's ragged whisper forged Will's fury into hard, cold steel. Stealthily he moved into position and waited for his chance.

Raul laughed, and Will had to fight down another surge of deadly rage. He quieted his raging emotions just in time to hear Raul's next words.

"That's the beauty of it all. You aren't my daughter."

≈ ≈ ≈

Hard on the heels of so many other gut-wrenching disclosures, the revelation slugged Robyn deep into her solar plexus.

For a moment she couldn't breathe. Everything around her started to blur. *Raul wasn't her father*? How was that possible?

With a sneer, Raul provided a quick explanation.

"Oh, you did contact the right man – your real father – in the first place. You have no idea how excited Raul was, so excited that he had a fatal heart attack. But not before he'd told me all about you – including your Key West health club and his plans to reunite with you. I was sorry to see my partner go. He was wonderful at enticing investors. But he was also far too sentimental. He would never have agreed to use his oldest daughter to further my business plans.

"I, of course, have no such reservations."

His smile glittered with a calculated pride that made Robyn cold in places already chilled through and through.

"Since he died at his Cordoba ranch, it was nothing to hide his death and take over his identity, at least while I was in America. People had always said we could pass for brothers."

His lip curled. "If not for your stubbornness – and Sergei's idiotic obsession with you – the plan would have worked perfectly. It would have been easy to find another woman, any woman, with another business through which he could launder his millions. But no."

He shot an angry look at the Russian's still motionless body. "The fool had to have you."

"You're – you're Eduardo De Guzman?" Robyn whispered in horror.

The man who wasn't her father waved his hand impatiently. "Forget who I am. Yes or no? Will you divorce Will Ryder and marry Sergei? Think carefully, *mi amor*." He gave the endearment a sarcastic twist. "Whether you and Izzie leave here alive tonight or not depends on your answer."

Robyn's throat dried up. She wasn't sure she could get any answer out, much less the one this murderer wanted to hear.

She swallowed. A loud scraping overhead startled her. The heavy stationary bike, still festooned with red ribbons, wobbled for a second and then hurtled over the side of the open staircase.

The machinery crashed onto Raul's shoulders and slammed him to the floor. The gun skittered across the carpet and under another machine. Instantly Robyn dived for it.

Her hand closed around the gun, and she scrambled to her feet. A flash of motion caught the corner of her eye and she whirled towards the base of the stairs, the gun raised.

She sagged with relief. "Will," she whispered raggedly. "It's you. Thank God, it's you."

A groan came from where Raul was pinned by the machine. He struggled to wriggle out from under it, but Will was too fast. He grabbed a skipping rope hanging on the wall and pounced on Raul, binding his hands behind him and to the bicycle's crossbar. He crossed to where Sergei lay unconscious on the floor and trussed him in a similar manner.

Satisfied that neither man could escape, Robyn lowered the gun. Will opened his arms and she stepped into them without hesitation. As his solid warmth closed around her, she started trembling all over. How close she'd come to losing him – to losing everything that mattered.

"Will, I – "

"Get me out, please!"

Will and Robyn sprang apart and rushed to the leg press where Izzie was still trapped. They each removed weights from either side then Will shoved the safety bar in place to allow Robyn to pull her out. Izzie collapsed in a tear-sodden, sweaty bundle on the floor.

As Will called 911, Robyn wrapped her arms around her sobbing friend. The apricot scent of her skin, heightened by sweat, tickled her nostrils. "It's okay, Izzie. It's okay. The police are on the way."

Izzie only sobbed harder. "I'm so sorry," she cried. "I didn't mean – I never knew they were going to kill Vince. I just . . ."

Suddenly the apricot scent and Izzie's words came together in a shocking realization. A moment passed before Robyn realized she was digging her fingers into Izzie's shoulder. "What about Vince?" she demanded harshly.

Izzie sniffed and tried to wriggle away from Robyn. "Raul said he would marry me. He'd invest in the health club and we'd all be rich. Rich, Robyn, rich? Don't you understand?"

She shook her head. "But you had to dump Will – that was all. No one was supposed to get hurt. That's what the kidnapping was all about – once Will was arrested, you were supposed to dump him, and then go for Sergei. It would have been so easy if only you hadn't loved Will so much."

Robyn's throat clogged with disbelief. Her gaze hardened. She shook Izzie. "What about Vince? Who killed him?"

"I didn't know," Izzie wailed. "Sergei wanted to plant more evidence against Will, so he killed Vince and wrote that confession note. When I found out, he beat me up and threatened to kill me if I didn't stay quiet. I . . .I wanted to say something, but after he killed Ralph too . . ."

Robyn backed away from her friend in horror. "You and Ralph? You were both in on it too?"

Izzie raised her tear-stained face to Robyn. "Only the abduction, Robyn. No one was supposed to get hurt."

Robyn stood up. "No one was supposed to get hurt? You call kidnapping me from my wedding and framing Will for it not hurting anyone? You . . ."

The slam of the outside door and the thud of several pairs of heavy boots across the lobby interrupted her. Then Will's hand slipped around her waist and drew her stiff frame close.

His lips brushed her forehead. "Leave her, Robyn. The police are here. They'll take care of it."

≈≈≈

It was close to two a.m. before Will and Robyn left the club, together. The court order keeping them apart was still technically in effect but no one raised a protest.

Officers from Key West PD had arrived first, followed quickly by detectives on the night shift. Fifteen minutes later, Special Agent Rolland, looking as if he'd just rolled out of bed, came rushing in, along with Jamieson from the sheriff's office.

Raul – or Eduardo De Guzman – and Sergei when he regained consciousness -- attempted to bully their way out of the situation, loudly demanding immediate access to a lawyer. But Izzie's tearful confession, as well as statements from Will and Robyn, saw the trio swiftly led away to jail. Crime scene investigators were at work in the club now, and there was no longer any reason for Will and Robyn to remain.

Robyn, suddenly exhausted, handed Will the keys to her car. "You drive."

Will got in and started the car. He glanced at her. "Home?"

"Home."

They streets got quieter as they drove away from downtown in silence. The waning moon hung high overhead in the clear dark sky. Robyn didn't want to dwell on what had just happened, but she couldn't help it. She was still reeling from the disclosures that had knocked her world on its head.

Her father, an imposter. An imposter who was willing to kill, maim and destroy to get what he wanted.

Her best friend and maid of honor - a kidnapper who'd worked to undermine her marriage all the time she'd pretended to be concerned.

Betrayed by them both, but worst of all, betrayed by her own childish desire to be reunited with the father she'd dreamed about all her life. A desire that had blinded her to his faults, to the inconsistencies and other clues that should have made her see the truth about him, and about Sergei.

"I'm so sorry," she said finally, the words coming out in an anguished rush. "Sorry I didn't believe you right from the start. Sorry about Vince and Mark. If only –"

"Stop right there."

She turned to look at Will. In the dark interior of the car, he looked pale but serious.

His gaze on the road ahead, he continued. "No one's sorrier about Vince's death than I am. But you can't blame yourself. You had no way of knowing that Raul wasn't your father."

"But I should have known." Robyn bit her lip to keep back the tears that threatened to fall. "I should have known from the little things, everything from the fact that you didn't like him, his deep hatred of you for no apparent reason, his lack of interest in my mother's grave, or my mother for that matter. But no, I wanted a father so badly, I was willing to overlook almost anything. Even when you told me he tried to buy you off before the wedding, I didn't want to believe you. I had to have my precious father."

For a long moment, Will said nothing. Then, "Maybe it would have been different if we both hadn't tried so damn hard to protect each other from the truth. If I'd told you

267

the first time Raul tried to buy me off. If you'd told me that Sergei proposed. But we didn't. Neither of us believed we were strong enough – our love was strong enough - to face the truth."

Robyn reached for his right hand, her cold fingers curling around his warm ones, finding the solid comfort touching him always provided. "But we were strong enough, weren't we?" she said quietly. "I guess that's the good part."

"Yes." He turned his head to look at her, even a quick gaze setting off a flicker of warmth deep inside her. "And that Eduardo De Guzman isn't your father. Even he admitted your real father would never have done the things he did. Which reminds me. There was a reason I came looking for you tonight."

"A reason?"

"It wasn't just dumb luck I was there. No, I found the phone number for your father's ranch in Cordoba. Sam speaks Spanish, so I got her to phone."

"And?"

"A little girl answered. When Sam asked for Raul Leopoldo, the girl started to cry and kept saying the same thing over and over again. *Papa murio. Papa murio.*"

"Papa is dead?"

"Yes. Then a woman came on. She said Raul wasn't there, but Sam said she sounded scared. When she pressed her and tried to ask about what the little girl had said, the woman hung up."

"So?"

"Soooo." Will stretched out the word. When he turned to look at her again, he was smiling. "So I think you not only had a father who loved you right up to the end, but there is a half-sister in Argentina who will want to meet you."

The tears she'd been trying to hold back started to stream down her face. She squeezed Will's hand and leaned over to kiss his stubbled cheek. "Thank you for sticking with me through everything."

He held her gaze, his eyes shining like the clear blue waters where the Atlantic Ocean meets the Gulf of Mexico they could see from their house. "For better or for worse," he said. "Wasn't that what we promised?"

Gently he freed his hand from hers and wiped the tears from her left cheek. "We weathered the worst together, right?"

The lopsided grin she had loved from the start lit up his haggard face and drove the darkest shadows from her heart.

"Right."

Smiling through her tears, she grabbed his right hand again and raised it in a pretend toast.

"To better times ahead," she whispered. "Together."

Thank you for reading.
Please review this book. Reviews help others find
Absolutely Amazing eBooks and inspire us to keep
providing these marvelous tales.

If you would like to be put on our email list to receive
updates on new releases, contests, and promotions, please
go to AbsolutelyAmazingEbooks.com and sign up.

About the Authors

Although fraternal twins born in Canada, Norah-Jean and Susan spent their lives apart. Susan has lived in Canada and on both US coasts and the Midwest. She was an Operating Nurse assisting in hip replacements to heart surgeries. As a traveler, she has experienced over 50 countries (still more to go). But being a Mum was her favorite job.

Norah-Jean has spent her working life in Ontario, Canada, as a newspaper reporter, freelance writer and editor, and fiction author. She has published five novels, *Outrageous, Blue Dawn, Crazy in Chicago, Alien's Daughter and Night Secrets.* Her inspiration has come from thrills and chills in places as far flung as Timbuktu, West Africa; Sydney, Australia; and down the street from the Shakespeare Festival in Stratford, Ontario. She has a loving husband, and three grown children who keep returning to the "empty nest" despite her best efforts to shoo them away. Fate then brought the girls together again in Key West.

Did we mention that Susan is 6 ft. tall and Norah-Jean is five ft. tall?

Norah-Jean Perkin   Susan Haskell

ABSOLUTELY AMAZING eBOOKS

AbsolutelyAmazingeBooks.com
or AA-eBooks.com